CONTENTS

CHAPTER 1

The thunderstorm came at dusk. It had been threatening all afternoon with dark clouds racing across the sky from Collinsport Point to the lighthouse at the extreme other end of the cove where Collinwood was situated. The ocean had taken on a restless, angry mood with large, foam-flecked waves sending most fishing and pleasure boats to safe mooring. There was a strange silence in the air not usual in Maine in this vibrant late June when all nature came alive with sound and color. It was tense! A pause and perhaps a warning of strange things to come!

At least, that was how Victoria Winters felt about it. The pretty, dark girl had put on a raincoat and taken her umbrella before leaving Collinwood to stroll to the cliff in the eerie premature darkness which the approaching storm had brought. There was something in her nature that made her enjoy defying the elements and braving the sinister and unpredictable threats of the most terrifying of all nature's displays, the thunderstorm.

It had been an exciting day with all of them packing to leave for Vermont, and this was a fitting climax to it. She walked swiftly in the dark, uncanny silence, following the path along the steep cliffs to her favorite spot for solitary contemplation. Far below to her left the angry waves dashed against the rocky shore and behind her loomed the rambling main house of Collingwood,

BOOK EIGHT

WILL THE CURSE OF ANGELIQUE DESTROY BARNABAS' LOVE FOR A BEAUTIFUL MOVIE STAR?

Barnabas meets Rita Glenn, an actress whom he had known in London, when she is making a movie at Collinwood. Although they have not seen each other for several years, Rita soon discovers that her love for Barnabas is still strong, even when Barnabas tells her of the terrible curse upon his life.

But after Rita tells him that she knows someone who may be able to cure him, eerie things start happening to her. And then she begins to wonder if Angelique isn't in some sort of weird battle with her—a battle for the very soul of Barnabas Collins!

Hermes Press

Published by Hermes Press, an imprint of
Herman and Geer Communications, Inc.

Daniel Herman, Publisher
Troy Musguire, Production Manager
Eileen Sabrina Herman, Managing Editor
Alissa Fisher, Graphic Design
Kandice Hartner, Senior Editor

2100 Wilmington Road
Neshannock, Pennsylvania 16105
(724) 652-0511
www.HermesPress.com; info@hermespress.com

Book design by Eileen Sabrina Herman
First printing, 2020

LCCN applied for: 10 9 8 7 6 5 4 3 2 1 0
ISBN 978-1-61345-213-4
OCR and text editing by H + G Media and Eileen Sabrina Herman
Proof reading by Eileen Sabrina Herman and Theresa Halvorsen

From Dan, Louise, Sabrina, Jacob, Ruk'us and Noodle for D'zur and Mellow

Acknowledgments: This book would not be possible without the help and encouragement of Jim Pierson and Curtis Holdings

Printed in Canada

THE DEMON OF
BARNABAS COLLINS
by Marilyn Ross

a period piece now. And far to the rear of it, almost hidden by the barns and outbuildings was an even older house, which Elizabeth's cousin from England, Barnabas Collins, had rented.

Thought of Barnabas brought a small smile to Victoria's face. She was fond of the cultivated gentleman from London and knew his likes. He also had a feeling for the unusual, and she was sure he must share her own enchantment for the strangeness of this moment before the breaking of the storm. Barnabas had a perception and a flair for such things.

She came to a halt at the very summit of the cliff, where it jutted out high above the rough waves.

Victoria stared up at the dark sky with her nerves on edge. There was a distant, low rumble of thunder and she felt a single drop of rain strike her cheek. It could only be a matter of minutes before the storm burst in full fury. A feeling of guilt came over her as she realized how worried Elizabeth and Carolyn would be about her. Neither of them had the same intense interest in electrical storms as she, and they would be frightened for her out alone on this uneasy night. She was taking a risk, she supposed. People were often killed in such storms.

Especially dangerous were high places such as this summit on which she stood. But, while she knew it was wrong, she could not resist the temptation of it. She could only hope that Elizabeth would not be too greatly alarmed. Once the storm had begun and she'd seen some of its display she'd return to the house and let them know she was safe. Then she might even go on to have a brief conversation with Barnabas before she left. She enjoyed his company and would miss him during the long summer holiday in Vermont.

A low rumbling came again to send a tingling through her. She stared out across the angry ocean with a rapt expression. Collinwood had always fascinated her. The enigma of her own identity had made her take a special interest in the dark old mansion and its people. Elizabeth had accepted her as a daughter and sometimes she wondered whether or not she might actually be a Collins. Surely she had the typical Collins spirit and love of adventure. And that was one of the reasons she so disliked leaving the estate at this exciting time.

Collinwood had been rented by one of the major Hollywood film studios as the location for a historical romance about Maine, and as soon as they left in the morning, the advance party of the film company would take over the great house and make it the base of their operations for filming a movie. The famous stars, Rita Glenn and Clifton Kerr, would actually be living in Collinwood, as would director Brad Hilton and others in the movie. The rest of the Hollywood company would be living in the various summer hotels in the village as well as some of the private homes. All Collinsport was agog with the fact that it had suddenly become famous and everyone was anticipating the arrival of the Hollywood people, who would be remaining at least two months, or longer if the weather delayed their shooting schedule.

Victoria was disappointed. She would have liked to remain, just to be there when the film was being made, but Elizabeth had been firm. The arrangement was that the company was to have the house completely to themselves. The Collins family had rented a house in Vermont and they'd all spend the summer there—all except Barnabas and his mute servant, Joab, who would continue living in the old house, since it was not included in the rental agreement. Barnabas had requested that Elizabeth see to it that he was allowed to remain. Elizabeth had gone along with his wishes. Victoria was certain no one else would have had like influence on her. But then, Barnabas had such hypnotic charm it was not hard to understand why he was so easily able to persuade people to his way of thinking.

The first great bolt of lightning streaked across the ugly black sky. His roar of thunder fairly made the ground under her tremble, and Victoria experienced a thrill of delight.

Then the deluge came. The rain cascaded in great sheets, almost closing off all visibility. Victoria hastily opened her umbrella for protection from the deluge as she watched the storm develop. Another barbed flash of bluish yellow cut the darkness and the thunder assaulted her eardrums mercilessly. It was one of the most violent storms she's ever seen at Collinwood. Surely Barnabas must be staring up at the eerie sky watching it as she was!

Somehow the storm seemed to liberate her. The frustrations of the day were lost in the excitement of it, and when the lightning grew more faint and the rumble of thunder less loud she was somehow let down. The storm was on the wane, the sensation of it over. She could remain there only a little longer in the downpour before returning to the house. Sadness tinged her lovely face and she felt a deep sense of melancholy.

"Girl!" It was a male voice that called out to her, and one with deep bass authority. It came from close by.

She wheeled around in astonishment to peer out from under her umbrella in the direction from which the voice came. A tall, spare man with a balding head and a black patch over one eye stood close to her on her left. Victoria was startled because she had not thought of anyone being so near her or coming out on the hill in such a storm. Yet, the strange male figure could not be denied. There was a cynical smile on his long slab of a face, and his thinning hair was plastered across his skull from the drenching rain and a raincoat protected his body from the storm.

The slab face showed grim amusement. "You do have a voice, don't you?"

"Yes," Victoria barely managed to say in a tiny voice which she knew was ridiculous.

"Good," the tall man in tweeds and raincoat said, "So you talk and breathe and are a living girl. For a moment I suspected you were a phantom."

She smiled. "I'm Victoria Winters; I live at Collinwood. I promise you I'm no phantom, though it is claimed that spirits gather at this point of land." She was doing better, she decided with satisfaction.

The balding man nodded, seeming quite comfortable despite the pouring rain. "I've read about this cliff and the Phantom Mariner, who told the wives their husbands would not return from fishing voyages, so I was prepared for ghosts. In fact, I probably came out here in this storm in the hope of finding them."

Victoria looked at him earnestly. "I believe every very old place is haunted. I mean in a real way by the spirits of those who have lived there before. I'm sure Collinwood is."

The slab-faced man's single shrewd blue eye studied her thoughtfully. "You're an intelligent girl," he observed in his deep bass voice. "And a sensitive one. I agree with you completely about the ghosts in old places. And one does not need to have a visitation or anything of that sort. One senses the presence and feels the mood."

Victoria smiled. "Thank you. I mean, for saying that. I've always felt it but I've never heard it expressed so clearly before."

The tall man smiled indulgently. "I find you a charming girl," he said. "My name is Brad Hilton. I've come to Collinsport to direct the film. Please don't let that make a difference between us."

She laughed. "I'm not the autograph-collecting type, but I am pleased to meet you. I've been blue about leaving. We're all going in the morning."

"I know. I'm staying at the hotel in the village for tonight."

"I would have liked to meet Rita Glenn and Clifton Kerr and see how a movie is made," she went on.

The tall, balding man stared grimly out at the sea. "To paraphrase the late Sir Winston Churchill, a movie is made with an undue accumulation of blood, sweat and tears. You won't be missing much."

"I suspect you're trying to let me down easily."

"Not really," he said. "I've given my life to the industry and that's my experience. Rita Glenn is a pretty, talented girl but really no nicer than you as a person. Clifton Kerr is a neurotic, never without his doctor along, a tortured human being though a genuine talent. You're better off not meeting him."

Victoria smiled. "Thank you for the thumbnail profiles. I feel as if I know something of the company from an insider's point of view."

"And you do," the famous director assured her in his resonant tone. "The storm seems to be over except for the rain. I think I'll stroll back to my car. I left it in front of Collinwood. Why not walk back with me?"

"I'd like to," she said at once. "You can have part of my umbrella if you wish."

Hilton shook his head. "I like the rain. I have a farm in Ireland. Over there the rain is soft and soothing. I walk in it a lot."

"You really should meet Barnabas Collins," Victoria said seriously as they began walking back to Collinwood and the big limousine parked before it. "He'll be living here all the time you're making the picture and he's a very interesting person."

Hilton looked thoughtful. "He's the British cousin, isn't he? Mrs. Stoddard mentioned him. It was stipulated he be allowed to stay on in the old house. He's a scholar doing some kind of research, isn't he? I was against his remaining here. I suspected he'd be a nuisance."

"You couldn't be more wrong," she said. "He's a wonderful man."

The director gave her a curious glance. "I must say you sound very enthusiastic about him."

Victoria looked down, embarrassed. "I'm sorry. But I've found him a good friend and someone to talk to about things that don't interest the others." She gave Hilton a frank glance. "He's a lot like you."

He smiled wearily. "You know nothing about me, Victoria. We've just met."

"Still I feel I understand you and you understand me." she insisted.

The tall man with the raincoat over his shoulders seemed impressed by her words. He glanced at her again. "Do you believe in second sight?"

She hesitated. "I'm not sure."

"You should," he told her briskly. "I'm positive I have it.

It's the faculty for seeing events that happen at a distance or will happen in the future. Sometimes it comes as a warning of death with the appearance of shrouds, corpses and candle lights. Dogs and horses are believed to have it and they often show a weird knowledge of tragic events before they happen, manifesting fear and distress."

"I've read about second sight," Victoria said. "It's not always supposed to be a happy gift."

"It isn't," he agreed. "There are times when I consider it a curse. And I can tell you that I have had some strange feelings about coming here."

She stared up at his solemn face as he walked across the broad lawn with her. "You have some sinister feeling about Collinwood?"

"The idea of doing a film here makes me uneasy," he admitted. "And I don't know why. I suppose Clifton Kerr may be part of the answer. He's very difficult to direct and I'd rather not work with him."

"Perhaps you'll feel better about it when you actually begin work," she suggested.

"I hope so," Hilton said moodily. "And I'll tell you something else. When I had the impulse to come out here today I knew I would meet a girl on that cliff."

Victoria smiled in surprise. "You couldn't have known I'd be there!"

"It didn't have to be you," he said. "But I had the feeling I would encounter someone who had some important link with Collinwood." He paused and gave her a cynically amused glance. "I'll be frank. I was hoping it would be a lovely ghost. I expected it would be. Instead I meet an extremely alive and pretty girl."

"I'm sorry to disappoint you," she said. "You should have waited fifty or a hundred years. Then I would be exactly what you're looking for."

The director chuckled. "I'll settle for what I found," he said. "You've given me some interesting facts about the place and now I'll go back to my hotel and work."

They were near his car and had come to a halt. She said, "Wouldn't you like me to introduce you to Barnabas Collins?"

The man studied her with amusement again. "You are insistent about that. Perhaps I should meet him."

Victoria gave him no chance to change his mind but at once led him out by the barns to the area where the original Collinwood stood. The ancient building had an air of mystery about it on this dark and menacing evening. She was sure that the film director would be impressed by the house and its occupant.

As they walked she said, "There is an interesting old family cemetery out back. You must ask Barnabas to show it to you."

"Good. I may be able to use it for a background for some scenes."

"What kind of movie are you making?"

Hilton sighed. "It's a rather strange story. About a man who engages in the slave trade and makes his fortune in that despicable fashion. He comes back to his bride at Collinwood and brings one of the slaves with him. Gradually he loses his wife's love to a young Quaker who has come to live in Collinsport. He comes to believe the black man has cast a spell on him. He turns the slave out but it gives him no ease. When he learns his wife no longer loves him he sets out to sea in a small boat. He had hallucinations and imagines a schooner with slaves aboard is attacking him and he dies at sea, leaving his widow free to marry the Quaker."

"It is a strange story," she said.

"Not really as simple as it sounds," he assured her as they neared the old house. "There are other factors involved. I suppose you'd call it a story against slavery."

"Some of the early Collins men had a contact with the slave trade," she admitted.

"I've heard that," Hilton said. "And it was one of the reasons I decided to film in this area and use Collinwood."

They were at the entrance to the old house. Victoria mounted the steps and used the ornate knocker on the solid oak door. Barnabas never had callers until dusk and never showed himself during the daylight hours. He was a reserved man given to his research. Victoria had never seen his laboratory in the basement but she knew he spent most of the daylight hours there. Joab, his stout, deaf-mute servant zealously guarded the house until the evening.

As they waited, the rain continued to come down, but not as heavily as during the storm. Victoria had closed her umbrella and turned up her collar against the rain.

"His servant Joab is a deaf-mute," she told the film director. "So we'll have to wait for Barnabas to answer the door himself. And he is likely down in the cellar in his laboratory."

The tall man studied the stone house. "It has a lot of atmosphere. I'm glad you brought me over here," he said.

She smiled. "I told you that you'd enjoy it."

At that instant the door slowly opened and standing in the darkness of the hallway was Barnabas Collins. He stared at them for a silent moment. He was a tall man with a melancholy face. His high cheekbones, deep-set eyes and sallow skin gave his countenance a cadaverous cast. And yet, he was handsome. His thick black hair was streaked in disarray across his intelligent forehead and he wore a black Inverness coat with a cape and carried a cane with a silver wolf's head for a handle.

"Victoria," he said in his rich British accent. "I was not expecting you. I thought you had left."

"Not until morning," she told him with a smile. "I wanted to have you meet a friend, the director of the film, Mr. Brad Hilton."

Barnabas smiled, his lips parting to reveal glistening white teeth. "An unexpected pleasure," he said, extending his hand.

Hilton shook hands with him. "The same for me," he said. "I'll no doubt be meeting you often after we move in here tomorrow."

Barnabas continued with a thin smile. "May I be honest and say that it is an invasion which I'm not anticipating."

"We're not all that brash," the director assured him. "We're going to be working hard here. It's possible you may be able to give us a few tips about the family property. Our writer may want to talk with you."

Barnabas regarded him with those penetrating eyes. "I assume that Victoria explained I am of the English branch of the family, so I am also here at Collinwood as a visitor."

"Your accent betrays that," Brad Hilton said in his friendly way, the raincoat still draped over his shoulders as they stood on the steps in the drizzle and growing darkness. "But you still must know more about the family history than we do."

"I'll be happy to help in any way I can," Barnabas said. Then, as if he'd suddenly realized his oversight, he added, "But you must come in for a moment, both of you. At least I can offer you a glass of sherry."

The film director was quick to accept the invitation. "Thanks," he said. "I'd like to see the inside of the place. It's much older than the other house, I take it."

"This is the original family home," Barnabas said with great dignity.

Victoria stepped inside the dark hallway and the director followed her. She was at once aware of the dampness that seemed always to pervade the old house. She wondered that it did not bother Barnabas, but he appeared not to mind it.

He closed the door and they were cloaked in darkness. "Forgive the absence of lights," he apologized. "This house is not provided with electricity and I have been standing by the window in the darkness enjoying the storm. Did you see it, Victoria?" He asked this as he led them down the shadowed corridor.

"From the cliff," she told him. "That's where I met Mr. Hilton."

"And what a splendid place from which to view the spectacle of nature," Barnabas said. "I take it you also are interested in the violent moments of the elements, Mr. Hilton."

The director chuckled in the darkness. "I went out there in search of a phantom. And I found Victoria."

Barnabas led them through the wide double-doors of the living room and went forward to light the candles that Victoria knew were on the sideboard. He said, "I'd say you were quite lucky, Mr. Hilton. Phantoms don't always make such pleasant company." As he spoke he touched the candles alight to cast a faint glow over the room.

Brad Hilton stood by Victoria, his single eye taking in Barnabas. "You speak as if you've had some personal experience with phantoms, Mr. Collins. Am I being offered the opinion of an expert?"

Barnabas hesitated there a moment outlined against the glow of the candles. A noble figure in his caped coat and with a strange expression on his melancholy, high-cheeked face.

"I have some knowledge of spiritualism," he admitted. "It is a British vice, they say."

Hilton smiled. "I live in Ireland whenever I have any free time. I've learned a good bit about spirit lore over there. And the wee people who stalk the night and cause so much confusion."

Barnabas Collins nodded. "There are many beliefs concerning those that stalk the dark shadows," he said. "I have never inclined to any particular school."

"You are engaged in research," the film director said. "May I ask what type of work it is?"

Barnabas showed a blank expression. "My work is rather obscure, Mr. Hilton. I doubt if you would be interested in it. It has to do with both chemistry and metaphysics, which you will agree is a strange combination. Now, if you will both excuse me I will fetch the sherry." He bowed gracefully and left the room.

Victoria wondered what her new friend was making of the place. The rain could be heard dripping from outside, and the two candles barely gave the big room sufficient light to reveal the dusty and neglected condition of its elaborate furnishings. She had come to accept this state of things here, but she supposed the atmosphere must seem weird to an outsider.

Hilton moving slowly about the large living room examining paintings of long-dead members of the Collins family and the exquisite pieces of antique furniture with their liberal covering of dust. He paused in his tour of the room to turn to Victoria and smile. "You were right in saying this would interest me."

"I'm glad," she replied.

He made a gesture indicating all the room. "No film studio could duplicate a set like this. This is a room of the dead. It gives the feeling that no living person has been here for years."

"Your second sight at work?"

"Yes, if you like," he said. "This place gives me a strange sensation of tragedy and death."

"The Collins history has had its dark moments," she reminded him.

The tall director came across the dimly lit room to her. "And this Barnabas Collins," he said. "Doesn't he strike you as unusual?"

"In what way?"

He shrugged. "It's hard to put your finger on. Say it is in his aloofness. He seems to keep to himself even when he is talking to you. And then the touch of his hand. I never knew a human hand to be so cold."

Victoria said, "This house is cold and damp. He doesn't properly look after himself."

"So it seems," the director said thoughtfully, and resumed his tour of the musty room.

From a distance there came the sound of a dog howling, mournful and piercing. Victoria gave a tiny shudder. "That poor animal," she said. "Out on a night like this."

Hilton's single good eye fixed on her. "Don't you think it sounds like a wolf?" he asked.

"There can't be any wolves around here," she said. "It must be somebody's dog." As she finished speaking, the mournful howling cut through the rainy night once again.

"It has a bloodcurdling note," Hilton commented as he moved on to a door at the other side of the room and turned its handle to open it. When he swung it open he was faced by a stout, bulldog-faced man with glaring eyes. Hilton gave a small gasp.

"That's Joab," Victoria explained quickly, moving over beside the director in a protective gesture. "He's the deaf-mute I mentioned."

"And not very friendly, judging by his expression," the tall man said. He took a step forward but Joab shook his head and raised a clenched fist to warn him back.

The director turned to Victoria. "I guess we're not supposed to wander through the rest of the house on our own."

"I expect Barnabas has given him instructions," she apologized. "And Joab isn't one to make exceptions."

"That's certain," Brad Hilton said. "Sorry we disturbed you," he told Joab and closed the door again. Then he gazed around the candle lit living room. "I expect this is the most interesting room in the house anyway."

"It's the largest."

"Have you seen the others?"

"Just one or two of them," Victoria said. "When I call on Barnabas we usually sit in here and chat."

"Not what I'd call a cozy corner," he said. "I'm beginning to think that you enjoy making strange friendships—Barnabas and me, for instance."

She smiled. "I find you both engaging."

At that moment Barnabas came back into the room carrying a silver tray with a dusty wine bottle and two glasses. "Forgive my being so long," he said. "It took me a while to locate the vintage stock I wanted."

The director smiled. "I've been enjoying this room. It's a museum piece."

Barnabas poured the wine carefully. "Yes, I suppose that is the way it must strike you."

"And you feel differently about it?" Brad Hilton asked.

Barnabas handed Victoria her glass of sherry and then gave the director his. "Because of my family relationship with all that is here, it strikes me rather differently," he said.

Hilton held up his sherry. "Aren't you going to join us, Mr. Collins?"

Barnabas smiled in his melancholy way. "If you will excuse me, alcohol is not my drink, Mr. Hilton. But I do want you and Victoria to enjoy the sherry. I believe it is excellent."

Victoria sipped hers. "It is. I think you're so lucky, Barnabas. To be here when all the glamorous people arrive to make the movie. Clifton Kerr and Rita Glenn and all the rest."

Barnabas raised his heavy black eyebrows. "Did you say Rita Glenn?"

Brad Hilton nodded over his sherry. "Yes. She's our star. Is her work familiar to you?"

"Very familiar, indeed," Barnabas said with a slow smile. "It happens that I knew Rita very well when I was in London. She played on the stage there for several years."

Victoria's eyes sparkled. "Isn't that exciting!"

"I call it fortunate," Brad Hilton said. "Rita will find it hard to fill in her leisure time while she's here. Having an old friend will make it much more interesting for her." He raised his glass of sherry. "To your meeting with the lovely Rita again," he said, making a toast of it.

"Thank you," Barnabas said as they drank their sherries. "Rita is indeed a lovely young woman." And his eyes held a faraway, infinitely sad look.

CHAPTER 2

Rita Glenn's first view of Collinwood was of a spectral old mansion shrouded in fog. A blanket of misty grayness swirled about the proud old building and cut off all else from view. As the limousine which had brought her from the Bangor airport made its way along the bumpy cliff road she could see the point where the land ended, but the cove and ocean beyond were lost in a veil of fog. And from a distance there came the regular eerie groaning of the Collinsport foghorn. It was a bad beginning for the filming project at Collinwood.

Only the day before, she had deserted the warm sunshine of her Beverly Hills mansion to make the plane trip to New York. She'd stayed in Manhattan overnight, seen a Broadway show and then had taken an early morning plane to Maine. There had been delays in the landing at Bangor because of the fog, so she was not entirely surprised to find it worse along the coast.

Brad Hilton had sent a limousine for her as he'd promised. That was the one satisfying aspect of the venture. She felt she could count on Brad. He was a good director who looked after his people on and off the set. And she would need him to protect her from the egotistic Clifton Kerr, who was to be her co-star in the film. She'd worked with Kerr once before in Hollywood and it had not been a pleasant experience.

For one thing he was a neurotic and for another he possessed an incredible arrogance. He considered himself a great talent, and admittedly he was a good actor, but not of the stature he pretended. And to back him up in any unreasonable demands there was the sinister Dr. Lee Moreno, who was Kerr's personal physician as well as his manager. Moreno never seemed to leave Kerr's side, and while Rita had respect for the fact that he might be a good doctor, she felt he encouraged Kerr in his neurotic tendencies and was generally responsible for the star's being such a problem to handle.

Rita's spot in Hollywood firmament was secure. She'd first come to attention in a supporting role in a New York stage play. This had gotten her a Hollywood contract and a major part in a picture that had won an Academy Award. From then on her career had continued upward at a dizzying pace. Now she had five years of major starring films behind her, two years on the London and New York stages, and a film contract that would go on until she was more than financially secure. Still, she felt she had to be careful of the parts she took and the directors under whom she worked. She knew this picture would be a good one and the female starring role offered excellent opportunities. The only marring detail was her co-star, Clifton Kerr, and she was depending on Brad Hilton to keep things running smoothly and not let Kerr take any unfair advantage of her in stealing scenes.

At twenty-six Rita was the golden girl of her studio. Her blonde hair and tanned good looks gave her the appearance of the ideal outdoor American girl. Strangely enough, many of the parts she played were of a different type. In this film she was to play the young, sensitive wife who was not at all an earthy person. It was a tribute to her talents that she could adapt to almost any role.

She had paid little attention to the details of the location beyond the fact that it was to be in Maine and she'd need some warm clothes in case of sudden weather changes. A throat or nose cold could be expensive for a film unit with almost a hundred people involved when you included the technicians and local help. The foggy greeting made her apprehensive of how it would all turn out.

As the limousine came to a halt in front of the old mansion she saw the various studio trucks parked on the grounds, and the technical men were working in spite of the gray dampness. Brad Hilton came down the steps to greet her with a smile. She always felt his long face was more suitable to a prizefighter than a film director, and it was a fact that in his younger days he had been a boxer. It was then he had received the eye injury which had cost him the sight of his left eye.

Brad embraced her and kissed her cheek. "I was worried about your flight, Honey," he said. "I didn't know whether they'd be able to land."

Rita smiled up at him. "They came down whether they knew where the airport was or not. I guess they have a lot of this pea-soup weather in this section of Maine."

The tall director groaned. "Don't say such a thing, Rita. I'm counting on fifty days of sunshine and wrapping this up ten days ahead of schedule. I've got a country fair to attend in Ireland."

She laughed. "You and your Ireland! From what I hear you're more than three-quarters Polish."

Brad winced. "But it's that wee bit of Irish that rules me, Darlin'," he said in a mock brogue. And reverting to his normal tones he told her, "I'll see that your luggage gets in. I have a fine room on the second floor reserved for you."

"Couldn't you have found me something better at the local hotel?"

He shook his head. "I spent the night at the local hotel and I know. It's not nearly as comfortable as you'll find it here. And besides, living here will give you a chance to absorb the atmosphere of the place. You'll need that for the film."

She smiled at him as they mounted the steps. "I like the script."

"It's a broth of a story," he agreed. And with a knowing look he added, "And I have premonitions that we will make movie history here."

Rita arched an eyebrow. "Do you still believe in second sight?"

"More than ever," he assured her. "And I've added some ideas about phantoms and goblins. It has to do with living part time in Ireland."

"I knew it would eventually spoil you," she teased as they entered the big main hallway of Collinwood. At once she was struck by a large oil painting of a man of a long-ago era. For some reason she couldn't fathom, the strong, melancholy face seemed familiar to her.

Brad paused at her side and studied the painting with her. "How do you like it?" he asked.

"It's a handsome face, but sad," she observed, her eyes still fixed on the portrait. "I don't know why, but I feel I have seen it before."

The tall director chuckled. "I wondered if you'd notice."

She turned to stare at him in astonishment. "Notice what?"

"The portrait," he said. "It's a real old one. That's a painting of the first Barnabas Collins. He died about a century ago."

"Barnabas Collins," she repeated the name.

"And you've met the present namesake of the line," Brad went on. "I must say he looks enough like his ancestor to be his twin."

Rita turned to gaze at the portrait again. "Barnabas Collins! I knew him in London!"

"Of course you did," Brad said enthusiastically. "And I have news for you. He's right here at Collinwood, living in the old house a hundred yards or so from here. And he was glad to hear that you were coming."

The pretty blonde girl turned to the director in smiling amazement. "But it's incredible that I should meet Barnabas here. He was busy with some big research project in London when I last saw him five years ago. I can't imagine his coming to America and a small town like this."

"It's the place where his ancestors were born," Brad said, his good eye studying her seriously. "I guess he had an urge to come back and it's given him a place to work quietly. He has a lab rigged up in the cellar of the house. No one ever sees him except occasionally in the evenings."

She nodded. "It was the same in London. We never met during the day. But he would meet me backstage night after night."

"You make it sound as if you were pretty friendly," the director said.

Rita smiled demurely. "We were very friendly."

The tall man was surprised. "He didn't give me any hint of that, though he did seem glad to hear you were going to be living at Collinwood. The way you talk it must have been serious between you two."

"It was," she said with a sigh. "I was hoping he'd ask me to marry him."

"But he didn't."

"No. After a time I saw that he wouldn't. There seemed to be something troubling him, holding him back. I put it down to his work," she said with a grimace. "My pride wouldn't let me believe it was another woman."

"It couldn't have been. He's still not married. He's living here with a manservant to look after him."

Rita's face brightened. "That's hopeful news. When I was sure nothing was going to happen between us I left London. It was after I came back to New York that I got my film contract. If Barnabas had asked me to marry him I'd never have been a star today."

"Then it did turn out the right way," Brad said.

She shrugged. "I wonder. There are more important things

than being a celebrity. I truly loved Barnabas and I think he loved me. I don't know why it didn't work out."

Brad gave her a cautioning glance. "Don't go all romantic and mooning on me before the picture even starts rolling," he said. "I want you to have your mind on business."

She laughed. "Don't worry about that. I'm ready to give you my best. But I will be glad to see Barnabas again."

"And so you shall," he promised. "All in good time. I'll see you to your room. After you've freshened up, join me for lunch down here and we'll discuss the production together."

Rita was more impressed as she saw the rest of the fine old mansion. Everywhere, it was evident that the Collins family had settled for nothing less than the best, and she was astounded to learn from Brad that the house had forty rooms. Her own room was on the second floor at the front of the house, overlooking the ocean. It had a fine four-poster bed with canopy, and a white marble fireplace to contrast with its crimson walls.

"It's the best room in the house," Brad said, standing with her in the center of the big bedroom. "Elizabeth Stoddard uses it when she is here. I decided it had to be for you."

Rita offered him a grateful smile. "One of the things I've looked forward to about this film is working with you."

The director looked pleased. "It's going to be a fine film, Rita. We'll make it one. I hope you can manage without Blanche until she arrives."

Blanche was Rita's personal maid and dresser and she was coming on a later plane with the rest of the company. Rita had come a day ahead to have her extra evening in New York.

She hugged the copy of the bluebound script she was carrying and said, "I do miss her. She's become a kind of right arm. But I'll make do until she gets here."

"She should arrive this afternoon," Brad Hilton promised.

A sober look crossed the pretty star's face. "And when does Clifton Kerr arrive?"

Brad showed bitter amusement. "Not until tomorrow at the earliest. A special concession."

"So it's beginning already!" Rita exclaimed.

"Don't let it worry you," Brad Hilton said. "Remember you're going to have Barnabas Collins here to bolster your spirits. I'll be waiting for you to join me downstairs." With a friendly nod he left her, closing the door after him.

Mention of Barnabas again brought back a flood of memories of those days in London. She'd been enjoying her first stage success when the courtly man had presented himself backstage one evening after the performance and presented her with a bouquet and a box of candy. It was such an old-fashioned gesture she'd been touched and at once interested in the melancholy man with his formal evening wear and cape.

No one in London seemed to know much about him except that he frequented the night scene and theater world. He had been seen much in the company of many lovely women and there had been dark, whispered gossip concerning him and these lovely ladies, for several of them had come to violent deaths. While Barnabas Collins had not been charged with any of the crimes, the fact that he had been friendly with all of the unfortunate girls cast a black shadow over his reputation.

Rita had heard the stories and been warned by some of the older women in the cast, but on meeting Barnabas she promptly discounted the warnings. He was such a completely charming and kind person. Like many other people she knew, he had certain peculiarities. When they had midnight suppers after the theater he rarely ate or drank anything, but he made it up to her in interesting talk while she enjoyed the food. And he was an excellent dancer, especially excelling in the waltz. It was not uncommon for them to spend several evenings a week dancing at the Dorchester Hotel.

But she never saw him during the day, though she had several times pleaded with him to take her to Stratford-on-Avon. She wanted to visit the Shakespeare country with him because he was a Shakespeare scholar and seemed to have seen or known about all the greatest performances of the Bard in the past century. Often his knowledge of things past bewildered her. He would speak of the early 1800s as if he had lived in that period. And when she humorously chided him he would smile and say that his knowledge came as hearsay from a fond grandfather.

Perhaps the painting she had seen downstairs that so resembled Barnabas had been of that same grandfather, or even a great-grandfather. She must ask him when they met. The prospect of seeing him again filled her with happiness. Although she'd won fame in Hollywood, there had been no true romance in her life. Barnabas had come closest to her heart, and for some strange reason of his own he had chosen not to speak of his love for her.

Things might be different now. Meeting him here in America might offer a new light on their relationship. The fact that this house had belonged to the handsome Englishman's ancestors and she was surrounded by the cherished treasures of his family gave her a special feeling. She moved across to a vintage dresser with an ornate mirror and stared at the reflection of herself. She showed some weariness from her journey. She was not as fresh looking as she had been five years ago in London at twenty-one, but she was still a striking beauty and she hoped she might this time win the enduring love of Barnabas.

Realizing that she was keeping Brad waiting, she quickly put down the script and prepared for her shower. The bathroom attached to the old-fashioned bedroom was modern and obviously a recent improvement. After losing no time in the shower she donned a simple woolen dress of smart styling and stood before the dresser mirror putting on her make-up.

The fog was still heavy and the light in the room was poor. There was no view from her windows beyond the swirling gray dampness that had settled on everything. As she worked to complete her lips she suddenly sensed a presence in the room beside her. It was such a definite feeling that she paused with lipstick in hand, staring into the mirror with incredulous eyes to see who it might be.

For surely there had been a chilling stirring near her, and for an instant she almost had felt the pressure of cold fingers on her bare upper arm. She stood there motionless, not knowing what it meant. Then there was a sudden flooding of faint perfume in the air around her. The delicate scent of wild violets! As the perfume assailed her nostrils she was again conscious of an icy presence close by her. And from a distance, or perhaps from that very room, there came the soft echo of muffled, mocking laughter. Rita was stunned by the happening. Afraid to move, she searched the mirror for some sign of the intruder, then glanced hesitantly around her. Of course there was no one. The room was empty except for herself.

She was trembling, trying to tell herself she had imagined the whole business, but the perfume of violets was still strong in the air. She could not be mistaken about that. She stood there for a long moment trying to decide what it meant. Gradually the chill in the air vanished, as did the aroma of wild violets, and it left her unnerved.

Her hand was shaky as she used her lipstick again, but she did not try too hard with the rest of her make-up. She was anxious to hurry downstairs and tell Brad of her strange experience.

She left the room and made her way down the broad stairway to the lower floor. Brad had a table set for them in a small room at the rear of the big house, a kind of private dining room where they could talk. Like the rest of the house, it was shadowed because of the dark day and the fog. Brad was standing just inside the door waiting for her and she rushed to him and threw herself in his arms impulsively like a little girl.

"Brad, I had a terrifying experience," she exclaimed, pressing close to him.

His arm around her, he said, "You must have. You're trembling."

She looked up at him anxiously. "Don't tell me I imagined it!"

Brad smiled. "I can't very well do that before I know what you're talking about."

"I'm sorry," she said, drawing back from him, somewhat ashamed at her display of nerves.

"Sit down," he said, going to the table and drawing out a chair for her. "Tell me about it."

As they sat at the table having luncheon she explained what had happened. Her dainty, oval face wore an expression of incredulity. "Do you think this house is haunted, Brad?"

Brad looked thoughtful. "Very likely."

Rita stared at him. "You make it sound so casual!"

"It's a theory of mine. I believe all old buildings are inhabited by ghosts of the past. Every so often we become aware of them."

"I'm sure I must have a little while ago," she exclaimed. "I'm terrified."

Brad smiled gently. "I see no reason why you should be. You're assuming that all spirits are vindictive and dangerous. On the contrary, some are of the most gentle and sympathetic variety. I think yours falls in that category."

She put down her coffee cup. "Brad, I can't accept it! You discuss ghosts as if they were as normal as us having our meal here now!"

"I'm sorry," he said. "I suppose it comes from my living so much in rural Ireland. I can't expect you to see this with my eyes."

"I don't."

"Consider a moment," he said. "You say you felt a strange presence, a chilling in the air, perhaps the touch of cool fingers on your arm. You also say the air was filled with perfume, the smell of wild violets. Added to this was the conviction you'd heard soft laughter. Does that suggest a malevolent spirit? I'd say the contrary."

"Malevolent or not I didn't like it," Rita said unhappily. "I don't know whether I want to stay on in that room."

"I'll move you in a moment if you say so," Brad Hilton assured her earnestly. "But I think you'd be making a mistake. I feel you may gain from this experience if there truly is a spirit haunting the room. It could add to the dimension you will bring to your role."

Rita smiled wanly. "There's nothing in my contract specifying that I should take acting lessons from ghosts."

Brad sat back in his chair and laughed. "I say you're all right, Rita, as long as you keep your sense of humor."

"It seems I will need one," she said.

"I wouldn't think about the incident any more," Brad told her, becoming serious again. "It could be that you imagined it all. You're a very sensitive person and the atmosphere of this house undoubtedly has made a strong impression on you."

She gave a tiny shudder. "I promise you it has."

"It probably was nerves," he went on soothingly. "Nothing more than that. Try not to dwell on it. You have a big task ahead of you in this picture and you must apply all your energy to it."

"I know," she said. "What about Clifton Kerr?"

"What about him?"

"Are you going to allow him to indulge in his usual temperament, try to steal every scene for himself?" Rita asked. "I know his tricks too well. I worked in one picture with him and I vowed it would be my last."

Brad Hilton raised a placating hand. "I think I know how to handle Clifton as well as anyone," he said. "Just leave it to me."

"What about that Dr. Moreno?" she asked. "Will he be coming here?"

"He always travels with Clifton. You know that."

"Why?" she demanded.

"Clifton Kerr claims he must have him. You know his health isn't good—hasn't been since that time he went to Africa about ten years ago to make a jungle film. He got a fever almost as soon as he returned to Hollywood and until Dr. Moreno treated him he wasn't able to work."

"Moreno may be a good doctor," Rita admitted grudgingly, "but I call him a sinister person. He has a way of slinking around, and those dark glasses he wears day and night, and the influence he wields over Kerr isn't healthy."

Brad nodded. "I know what you mean. He's not only Kerr's physician now. He's also become his personal agent. He had complete control of Clifton Kerr's finances and career."

"I don't trust him."

"I'm not sure I do either," Brad said with a frown. "But Kerr is a big name and a giant talent. To get him we had no choice but to deal with Moreno. That's the way it is."

Rita said, "I think it's the doctor who causes a lot of the trouble. He puts Kerr up to some of the arrogant things he does."

The director shrugged. "Part of that could be shrewd press-agentry. Before Kerr's illness he was merely a competent young leading man. One of maybe thirty or forty. He didn't stand out from the crowd in any way. Now, because of the headlines, his temperamental stunts have made him a big name. Someone special! And by a strange coincidence his talent has also matured."

"You knew him before he contracted this illness in Africa then?"

"I used him in several films," Brad said. "He was a completely different person from the Clifton Kerr of today. He was quiet and unassuming then. When I first saw him after he came back from Africa I thought he would die within weeks. He was a skeleton and looked like an old man. He couldn't bear sunshine or even daylight. He would see no one except in the evening in a dark room."

"And Dr. Moreno brought him back from that condition?" she said, caught up by the story.

"Yes, and not until the studio had exhausted every other possibility. They had specialists flown in from the East and even from Europe. None of them were able to do anything for Kerr. They had come to the point of deciding to make a settlement of his contract and drop him from the fist of stars when Dr. Moreno presented himself and claimed that he could cure Kerr if he were given complete charge of him without interference."

"And they agreed?" she asked.

"After some hesitation," Brad said with a thoughtful look. "The studio ran a routine check on Moreno and the findings weren't anything they especially liked. It turned out he was a medical doctor and he had even practiced in Africa for a while. But he had come back to the States and gotten himself in some trouble that nearly cost him his license. After that he gave up a regular practice and started a kind of mental healing cult in Los Angeles. You know how they go for crazy swamis in our town."

Rita smiled ruefully. "Only too well."

"So Moreno prospered with his new homemade cult. He had some big names among his followers. But the police hadn't forgotten about his bad record and were keeping a close watch on his activities. It was then that he went to Kerr's studio and offered to cure him."

"And they were desperate enough to let him try," she said.

"That about tells it," Brad admitted. "As I heard it, they didn't really expect any results, but Clifton had heard about Moreno's offer and insisted that he treat him. He did, and the two became as thick as the proverbial thieves. Within a short time Clifton had put on enough weight to appear before the cameras and was showing up on the set in the daytime."

"But Moreno ruled him?"

"I suppose you could say that," the director said. "I can understand his being grateful to Moreno. And you have to give

Moreno credit for curing him, regardless of his reputation. No doubt he picked up a lot of information about tropical fevers when he was in Africa, and he happened to know just what was wrong with Kerr."

Rita sighed. "It's a strange story, and it seems my instincts were right in judging Moreno as a shady character. That's what he is."

Brad smiled. "You're probably right. I have no doubt he's convinced Kerr that he can't survive without him. Kerr has become a definite neurotic, always terrified of relapsing into his old sickness again. Moreno undoubtedly plays on his fears and takes more than his fair share of Kerr's earnings for his services as physician and manager."

Rita said mockingly, "And that, kiddies, is the end of a rather ugly story." She got up from the table.

Brad rose with her. "It's not all that bad," he said. "Kerr has become a famous star and is earning fabulous money."

"And it does him no good," Rita said. "A lot of the time I don't like this business. And until we finish working here I'm depending on you to protect me from Kerr and his doctor friend."

"You can count on it," Brad said warmly. "Why don't you fill in your afternoon by going over and seeing your friend from London?"

They had walked out to the hallway. She said, "But you told me Barnabas was always busy during the daytime."

"He usually keeps out of sight, working on his experiments," Brad agreed. Then his face took on a knowing smile. "But judging from the way he reacted when I told him you were coming, I have no doubt he'd be glad to put aside his work for an hour or two for a reunion with you."

Rita smiled. "Where did you say his house was?"

"The old stone building just beyond the barns," the director told her. "You can walk there in a few minutes, but you'd better put on a heavy coat. It's damp outside and Barnabas doesn't keep the house overly warm."

"I have a coat upstairs," she said. "I'll get it."

"Perhaps you can persuade Barnabas to come over and have dinner with us," Brad suggested. "Tell him I'd enjoy talking to him again."

Rita went up and got the tweed coat she'd brought with her for the uncertain Maine climate. Everything seemed normal in her room and there wasn't a hint of the aroma of wild violets that had so upset her earlier. She began to wonder if Brad's theory wasn't right—that she had let her nerves take over and imagined the whole business.

She went down the broad stairway and out into the foggy afternoon not at all certain she was doing the right thing. She knew that Barnabas was dedicated to his work and she worried about intruding on him during the day. But to counter this, they had not met for a long while and he was apparently working on his own and free to do as he wished.

She walked quickly around the big house and the parked studio trucks in the direction of the outbuildings. Leaving the activity of the technical personnel behind her, she continued on through the fog-shrouded field in the direction of the old stone house, whose lines were only vaguely visible in the heavy mist.

The ground was wet and she regretted not having worn something heavier than her light, open-mesh shoes, but she went on until she reached the entrance of the old building. The front door was a fraction ajar and so she decided to mount the steps and go in. She did so, a little awed at the antiquity of this truly ancient building.

As she stepped into the dark hall she called out, "Barnabas!"

She was about to call out his name again when she heard a step from behind her, and before she could turn, rough hands had gripped her throat and she was being dragged back!

CHAPTER 3

Rita screamed as the hands tightened on her throat. Then she found herself out on the steps in the fog again with a stocky, strange-looking man glowering at her. Shaken by her experience, she stood there staring at him and trembling. Her hand caressed the lovely throat that had been so roughly assaulted and she tried to make some sense of the situation.

This squat, ugly man with his close-cropped gray hair and stubble of gray beard had literally dragged her out of the house by the throat. He stood glaring at her with his odd pop-eyes with their reddish veins and making guttural sounds. Had she not been so mesmerized by terror she would have turned and fled.

As it was she remained there, stunned by his actions and menacing appearance. At last she found a voice to say, "How dare you do that? I'm a friend of Barnabas Collins."

The squat man's grim, square face continued to show hostility as he made other snarling noises, and gestured with one of his powerful hands for her to get off the steps and leave.

Rita frowned. "Mr. Collins will take you to task for the way you've behaved towards me. I'm a friend of his. He wants to see me. Don't you understand?"

The brutish man's response was to snarl and wave again for her to go. She saw that there was to be no reasoning with him.

If Barnabas was somewhere in the depths of the old house out of hearing, there was no hope of getting in touch with him now. To remain and argue with this seeming madman was much too risky.

"Very well," she said, her eyes on the ugly, beard-stubbled face as she backed down the steps. "I'll go. But Mr. Collins will hear of your behavior towards me and I promise you he won't be pleased."

With that she turned and hurried back across the field toward the barns and the main house. She felt frustrated, frightened and more than a little unhappy. She had so looked forward to seeing Barnabas again and her reception at the ancient stone house had been anything but pleasant. Her throat still ached from the pressure of those powerful, calloused hands.

She walked on through the wet fog reaching Collinwood where the various technicians were busy. The area surrouding the big house was cluttered with snarling trucks, cables, lights and camera booms. Brad Hilton was planning to take some general locations shots around the old mansion in the morning if the weather cleared up. All this activity was directed toward that end.

Rita was familiar with the atmosphere and picked her way through the busy scene to the front entrance of Collinwood. When she went inside she found Brad Hilton finishing dictating a letter to his secretary. He was about to leave for the village.

Brad stepped out of the study to greet her. "What's wrong, Rita? Didn't your meeting with Barnabas go well? You look as white as a sheet."

"I didn't get to see Barnabas," she told him. "I was assaulted and ordered away by a horrible old man."

Brad gave a low whistle. "I should have warned you. That would be his manservant, Joab. He's a deaf-mute and has an ugly disposition."

"He grabbed me around the throat like a maniac," she complained, "and literally dragged me out of the house!"

The director looked alarmed. "He didn't do your throat any real harm, did he?"

Rita grimaced. "I'd call it only superficial, physically. But it was terrifying. And when I asked to see Barnabas he snarled at me and gestured for me to leave."

"No doubt Barnabas has given him strict orders not to allow anyone to disturb him and this fellow has taken them too literally. It's really my fault. I know Joab acts as a sort of guard around the place and I shouldn't have let you go there alone."

"I agree," she said. "You shouldn't have."

Brad stared at her, concern on his face. "You don't know how badly I feel about it. I'm positive Barnabas will feel equally upset when he hears what happened."

"I'll not go back there again alone," she said.

"I wouldn't think of allowing you to go," the director told her. "I'll see that a message is sent over to Barnabas after dinner so that he'll know you're here. He can come over here to see you."

She looked up into his battered face unhappily. "It's not a very good beginning, is it, Brad?"

He patted her arm. "You mustn't allow it to upset you. I have to go to the village to see about some equipment. We'll have dinner and discuss the script together when I get back."

Left on her own, Rita felt restless and disconsolate. She went upstairs to her room and skimmed through the script for a while, but the continual bleating of the foghorn distracted her and she could not seem to concentrate. Putting the script aside she left her room and began wandering through the upper portion of the old mansion.

Brad had told her it had about twenty rooms in the beginning and additional wings had been added through the years until the house became double its original size. The others of the company should arrive by evening if the fog didn't delay their flight and at least she would then have the company of her maid and dresser, Blanche. The unpleasant incident which had accompanied her attempt to visit Barnabas had put her in a depressed mood.

She began to feel the whole project might have been a mistake for her. It was only a short time before her co-star, Clifton Kerr, and the sinister Dr. Moreno arrived and they would add to the complications. She had reached the third floor of Collinwood and an area which had plainly not been in use for some time. An open door along the corridor invited her to enter and she found herself in what was plainly a storage room. There were ancient trunks and bags piled high in every direction. And cardboard boxes tied with stout cord gave off the musty odor of age. The ceiling of the room slanted at the outside and its single window was set in a little. She found a path through the stored goods to reach the window and peer out.

The panes were dust-covered and a spider had constructed a sturdy web at one corner of the sill and established his lair there. He waited immobile and malevolent in the center of the neat web for victims, the dried-out shreds of flies and other insects in its precise pattern giving evidence of his thoroughness. Rita avoided the web as she stared down below, a shiver of revulsion running through her.

Leaving the window, she turned to give her attention to the trunks and other contents of the room. The murky light offered through the window and the door opening on the corridor made it difficult for her to see clearly. On a bright day it might have been different. But at this time the heavy fog was obscuring everything.

As she gave the trunks a closer inspection she saw that one of them had been left open with its lid swung back. An ancient newspaper, long turned crisp and yellow, which had lined its top was thrown to one side. Looking into the trunk, she saw that it was filled with women's clothing of another era—a long-ago era at that! The sight of the old-fashioned dresses fascinated her, as did the odor of mothballs and pepper placed in the trunk to preserve the clothes from moths.

Impulsively she drew a dress up out of the trunk. It was the one which had first caught her attention. A party dress of the late eighteen-hundreds, it appeared to her. She held it up and even after all the long years of neglect it had a faded beauty. Its cut was to suit that other day with full bosom and narrow waist descending to a flowing long skirt line. It was of blue silk and must have cost a great deal when it was new. As she held it before her she could see it gracing some long-dead beauty with the flowing skirt whirling to a Viennese waltz!

And it was while she held the dress up before her conjuring this vision that she again experienced the intrusion of another presence. An unseen presence! The air took on that particular chill that she had first experienced in her bedroom and she could almost feel a body moving past her. But most startling of all was the sudden scent of wild violets that filled the musty air of the storage room.

The perfume was too strong to be ignored in the face of the murky room's musty odor. With a tiny gasp Rita allowed the dress to drop and tumble in a heap on the top of the trunk. Wide-eyed, she stared around her for some other manifestation of this eerie intrusion, but there was none, although the scent of wild violets continued to cling in the air.

It was beyond her understanding, this second similar psychic experience in such a short time. She hurried out of the storage room, pausing to gaze back inside from the corridor. There was no hint of motion or of anyone in there, yet she was sure she had not been alone. Someone had come to stand by her. The feeling was too real to be ignored.

Deciding she wanted to be alone no longer, she made her way down to the lower level of the house. It was only a few minutes later that the bus arrived from the airport with some of the lesser names of the acting company and the rest of the technical staff. A number of them were going to live at Collinwood, so the house became a hive of activity as they were allocated rooms. Rita was happy to see the comfortable, buxom figure of her maid, Blanche, appear in the front doorway of the old mansion.

She rushed forward to greet the older woman with a smile. "I'm so glad you're here, Blanche," she said. "I've been lost without you."

Blanche was fiftyish, serene and competent. She had been a maid and dresser to several stars before she'd come to work for Rita. Years in Hollywood had toughened her to handle almost any situation.

"We'll soon be comfortably settled in," Blanche said. "Though I must say the whole countryside looks bleak and forbidding to me."

"They say it is lovely on a fine day."

"Then, let's hope we soon get a lot of them," Blanche said. "Or all those preparations they're making out there won't come to much." She was referring to Brad's camera and lighting set-ups.

"There is a small room right next to mine," Rita said. "You're to have that. I'll show you."

She took the older woman upstairs and within a few minutes Blanche had taken over and was putting everything to rights. Rita at once felt much less lonely and was happier about it all.

Later, when Blanche was helping her dress for dinner, she told her about Barnabas. "You remember Barnabas Collins, whom I met in London."

Blanche looked unimpressed. "I can't say that I do, miss. You know I wasn't with you in those days."

Rita smiled into the dresser mirror as she sat there in a low-cut dinner dress, allowing Blanche to style her hair. "I do keep forgetting," she apologized. "But you have heard me talk about him."

"I have," Blanche said, busy with Rita's blonde hair.

"He's the handsome Britisher I thought about marrying," Rita reminded her.

Blanche sighed. "If you'll pardon me saying it, miss, it's been my experience that the happiest marriages have been made within the profession."

Rita's attractive face looked piqued. "You're telling me I won't be happy unless I marry an actor."

"I'm giving you the benefit of my experience," Blanche said firmly as she worked at Rita's hair. "You can take it or ignore it."

The star stared into the mirror dreamily. "This once I think I'll ignore it, Blanche. I'm sure I would be wonderfully happy with Barnabas as my husband."

A rueful smile crossed the older woman's face. "I expected you to say something like that, miss. Where romance is concerned there isn't any common-sense. And maybe there shouldn't be any."

Before Rita could make any reply there was a knock on the door from the hall. Blanche went to answer it and Brad Hilton was standing there smiling, a small package in his hand.

He stepped into the room and said to Rita, "You look ravishing tonight. I can hardly wait for you to join us at dinner." He offered her the package. "Something for you."

Rita had gotten up to greet him and she took the package with an inquisitive look on her pretty face. "What is it?"

Brad chuckled. "Open it and see."

She untied the ribbon of the gift-wrapped package quickly and removed the outer covering to reveal a box with the label: New England Violet Perfume.

"Oh, no!" she gasped.

He laughed. "Yes. I found it in one of the gift shops in Collinsport. The girl assured me it's a New England product and made from genuine violets. So I decided to get it for you."

Rita had opened the stopper of the tiny bottle and the aroma that exuded from it was almost identical with the one she had experienced on those two mystifying occasions.

"Thank you," she said. "It's lovely."

"I'll see you at dinner." Brad smiled and then he left.

After he'd gone, Rita debated whether to use the perfume or not. As it happened, she'd not chosen any for the evening before he came by. Now was the moment of decision. In a real sense, the scent of violets was frightening to her, reminding her of those eerie moments. On the other hand, the purchase of the perfume had been a generous impulse on Brad's part, and no doubt it would please him if she used it.

She smiled at Blanche. "I guess this will be my perfume for the evening."

"It smells lovely," the older woman said. "And it's sort of suitable to the atmosphere of this old house."

"I think you're right," Rita agreed quickly, although she did not tell her of her strange experiences. Perhaps she would later.

Downstairs she shared the private dining room with Brad and two of the main supporting players in the movie. One of them, C. Stanton Shaw, was a wizened English actor with a fine reputation for his portrayals in character roles. The other, David Billings, was a young man who had trained at the Pasadena Playhouse on the West Coast and had starred in television before moving on to film parts. He was to be the second male romantic interest in the film. He was a blonde, willowy youth with a kind of male prettiness which Rita did not admire but which seemed to gain him a lot of fans.

At the table Shaw asked, "Will Kerr be staying here at

Collinwood?"

"No," Brad said. "He prefers complete privacy. He's arriving with his doctor and entourage on his yacht, which will be docked at the wharf on the estate. He'll live aboard while he's making the picture."

David Billings tossed his head and said, "I'm sure we can manage very well without him here."

Shaw looked up from his plate. "I agree. Kerr can be difficult to get along with. And that Moreno is impossible."

"You needn't worry about them," Brad said, smiling across the table to Rita. "At least we have the most decorative star to keep us company."

"Bravo!" Billings exclaimed. In his brown turtleneck sweater and corduroy coat he looked very young.

Stanton Shaw glared at him, then gave Rita a knowing look. "Any of us who've worked with Miss Glenn before aren't worried about her," he said.

"When we've finished dinner I want to take you outside, Rita, and show you where I propose to do your first scene tomorrow," Brad said. "I'm sure you'll agree it's an ideal spot."

The swirling gray fog had not abated as dusk arrived and Brad led Rita out on the grounds of Collinwood. She put on her heavy tweed coat again and felt not a bit too warm. The director talked of the history of the ancient house and why he had chosen this site for his film as they strolled across the level lawn.

"As you know, slavery plays a big role in the film," Brad said. "And it is no secret in the area that some of the Collins money came from the slave trade."

Rita frowned. "Black gold, wasn't it called? I can't imagine righteous New Englanders engaged in such a traffic."

"They owned many ships and any cargo was of interest," Brad said wryly. "Even human cargo delivered at so much per head. But I will give credit to the Collins ancestors. They didn't dabble in the profitable trade as much as many of their neighbors."

"At least that's something," she said.

Brad Hilton came to a halt before a tall tree which had almost completely died. Of all its gnarled, outspread limbs only one of them showed any leaves. It stood there wreathed in fog like a gaunt, ghostly marker, and Rita stared up at it with a sense of awe.

"What do you think of it?" the director asked.

Her eyes were still fixed on the weird old tree. "It surely has a macabre air," she said.

"I think it will set the tone for the first scene we're doing tomorrow," Brad said with enthusiasm. "In it, Shaw, as an elder of the village, first informs you of your husband's activity in the slave trade. You are filled with disillusionment and horror. It's a strong scene and I think it should be played here."

She gave the director a rueful smile. "Let's say, the tree will put me in the right mood. It's one of the most grisly things I've ever seen."

"I can just picture it on the screen," Brad gloated. "It's bound to be terrific."

As he finished speaking, Rita heard footsteps approaching across the lawn and she turned to see who it was. Gradually the figure emerged from the heavy mist and her heart caught in her throat. The tall, broad-shouldered man, hatless and wearing an Inverness cape, at once made her think of London. It was Barnabas Collins who was coming to join them.

"Barnabas!" she said joyfully, taking a few steps to meet him.

The dark-haired, melancholy-faced man smiled at her in greeting. "Rita! I'm delighted to see you again. I heard you were coming." He took her in his arms and the kiss he planted on her lips was cool but still ardent, just as she remembered from London.

When he let her go she led him over to Brad. "You've met Brad, of course," she said.

Barnabas nodded. "Yes, I have had that pleasure. So you are already at work, Mr. Hilton."

The tall director nodded. "We have an expensive company. Time is money. I have been showing this old tree to Rita. I'm planning to use it as a background for a scene of despair. Appropriate, don't you think?"

Barnabas looked up at the tree with penetrating eyes. "It was a handsome tree once," he said seriously. "Even now in death it has a majesty."

"I agree," Brad said. "That's why I want to use it."

The man in the cape coat gave the director a knowing glance. "You will find much to remind you of death and age here, Mr. Hilton. If that is the message you have chosen to bring to the screen then this site is well-chosen."

Brad said, "That's partly the story I'm telling. There's also something of slavery in it and romance."

"Our family has torn out the pages referring to the slavery profits from the old journals," Barnabas said with a grim smile. "They have retained the money made but cast aside the guilt."

Rita spoke up, "Mentioning guilt, I have a complaint to make. I went over to call on you this afternoon and that servant of yours attacked me."

"Joab did?" Barnabas said, becoming concerned. "I can't imagine him acting so stupidly!"

"Dangerously," Brad corrected him. "He almost did Rita bodily harm. I'd say you should give the fellow a dressing down."

Barnabas nodded, his hand clenching his silver-headed cane until the knuckles showed white. "I have tried to explain to him, but he does not seem to have any judgment." He turned to Rita. "This distresses me!"

Rita smiled. "It's over now. I'm willing to forget about it, but I won't go near your place unless I know you're going to be waiting for me."

"It's most unfortunate," Barnabas said in his controlled, dignified way. "Joab is a deaf-mute, as you know. In addition, he is a trifle retarded. It is not easy to make him fully understand anything, but I will give him strict orders not to approach you at all."

"Is he as ferocious as that with everyone?" Rita wanted to know.

Barnabas sighed. "He can be brutal. But I require protection. You have no idea how many people try to interrupt me during the day when I'm engaged in my research, the type of research in which interruptions can waste a vast amount of time."

"I'll not try to see you in the daytime again," Rita promised.

"That would be best," Barnabas agreed. "I'm always deep in my lab in the cellar. It is soundproof and I have no idea what is going on outside. Joab has the full run of the house."

"I've warned my people not to bother you," Brad said. "And I don't think they will."

"And I'll ask Joab to improve his manners," Barnabas said with a small smile.

Brad turned to Rita. "I have other work to do, so I'll leave you two to talk. You no doubt have a great deal of catching up to do." He smiled. "Just don't forget there's an early call if the weather is right tomorrow and I don't want you looking tired for the close-ups."

"I'll remember," Rita promised.

Brad left them alone. As he vanished in the fog there was a moment of awkwardness between them. Then very gently Barnabas raised his hand and stroked her hair, which was damp from the mist.

"My golden girl has become a movie queen," he said quietly with a strange, sad expression on the high-cheekboned face.

She looked up at him with a smile. "It's not important to me, Barnabas. Believe that. All day I've been thrilled at the prospect of seeing you again."

"And I have looked forward to being with you," he agreed, more somber. "Things are still not exactly as I would wish. I'm shocked by what Joab did to you."

"I told you, it doesn't matter."

"It does to me," Barnabas said. "You must not come near the house during the daytime again. I cannot be responsible for him then."

"I only hope he doesn't get in trouble with any of the others in the company," she pointed out. "There will be so many around."

The man in the dark cape nodded. "I have been worried. Afraid that something of this sort would happen. I did not dream that you would be involved."

"Do you want to go inside?" she asked, indicating Collinwood.

Barnabas stood there in the growing darkness looking uneasy. "I don't think so. Not tonight," he said. "There will be others in there."

"Some of the company. Most of them are very nice people," Rita said. "I'm sure they'd like to meet you."

"Perhaps later," he said evasively. "I have a headache this evening. I do not feel up to conversation."

She stared up at him earnestly. "Barnabas, it is going to be different this time. We are going to see more of each other. Talk things out between us. Not just leave matters up in the air as we did in London."

His deep-set eyes met hers. "Rita, you know how fond I am of you, but you must not expect too much of me."

"I love you, Barnabas," she said softly, "and it is my hope that you also love me."

The tall, broad-shouldered Barnabas took her in his arms. "Try to understand that it is even more difficult for me than it is for you, and that whatever I do is for your good."

"If you leave me again I will find that hard to believe," she said.

But he ended her reproof by kissing her gently again, and once more she was aware of the coldness of his lips. They sent a tiny shiver through her and she was at once conscious of the coolness of the night. They had been standing in the fog a long time.

"You're trembling," he said, staring down at her. Then a curious look crossed his face. "That perfume!" he said. "Where did you get it?"

"Brad gave it to me. It's local," she said. "Wild violets. Do you like it?"

"Wild violets," he repeated. "Of course. That is why I noticed," he spoke as if to himself. Then giving her his attention again, he said, "It is a truly lovely perfume and it evoked some poignant memories for me."

She looked up at him with wide eyes. "It did?"

His face became gentle. "Long ago I knew someone who never used any scent but wild violets."

Rita was startled. She was on the verge of telling him of her two weird experiences in smelling the perfume of wild violets in the house but she hesitated to do so, wanting to hear first what he had to say.

"I find that interesting," she said. "Was it someone in London?"

Barnabas looked mysterious. "It was a long time ago. Really too long ago to remember."

He disappointed her by refusing to talk about it any more, and insisting she must be cold, he escorted her back to the front door of Collinwood. After promising to see her on the following evening he bade her a hasty goodnight and walked off into the fog. Rita entered the house in a troubled frame of mind. She had hoped to find a change in Barnabas, but he still appeared reserved and strained, as if afraid to declare his love for her. It worried and puzzled her.

Blanche helped her prepare for bed. Because she was tired, she fell asleep in the comfortable old fourposter almost immediately, but she was awakened in the middle of the night by a screaming from the grounds.

It took her a moment to realize where she was, then she sat up, staring into the darkness and listening to the screams repeated again and again.

CHAPTER 4

Rita pressed her hands against her ears to shut out the ugly sound, and after a moment the screams ended as quickly as they had begun. There was no sound from any other part of the house and she began to suspect that she could have been the victim of a nightmare. For some minutes she sat listening for any other noise from outside, but none came.

Deciding that it was nothing that should concern her, she lay back on the pillow and dropped off to sleep again in a few minutes. This time her rest was uninterrupted until morning. It was Blanche who woke her when she began raising the blinds and bustling about the room.

"A lovely sunny morning, Miss Glenn," her dresser said. "Mr. Hilton will be wanting you on the set early."

"I'm glad it is," Rita said, sitting up. "And it seems warmer."

"As warm as you can expect in Maine," the older woman said. "I have your bath drawn and ready."

Rita had finished her bath and was seated in a dressing gown at the breakfast tray which had been brought to her room, when there was a knock at her door. Blanche opened it and Brad Hilton came in, handsome in brown slacks, tweed jacket and beige cravat. He was solemn as he came to Rita.

"There was some trouble last night," he said.

At once she remembered the screams and her pretty face clouded. "What happened?"

"A strange attack was made on one of our script girls," the director said. "It happened after midnight."

"I was awakened then. I thought I heard screams."

"It was probably when the girl was being attacked," Brad said with a frown. "She came staggering back to the house in a dazed condition and woke the girl she was rooming with."

"Does she know who it was?"

He shook his head. "She's not really coherent about it yet. For the most part, she doesn't seem harmed except for a strange mark on her throat, and she complains of feeling terribly weak."

"She didn't see anyone at all?"

"No," the director said. "She'd been in Collinsport with one of the cameramen at a tavern called the Blue Whale. He dropped her off near the house when they returned but he didn't see her to the door. The attack happened after he started driving back to the village and before she reached the house. Someone came up behind her, according to her story."

Rita's face was pale. "At the time I was awakened by her screams," she admitted. "I thought I was having a nightmare."

"It was no nightmare," Brad said dryly. "The police have been here, and from what I heard from them this isn't the first such incident in the area."

"No?"

"No," Brad said seriously. "The constable at Collinsport told me there have been a series of such attacks. All in the night. And generally the victims have been young women who don't seem to be harmed except for this same mark on their throats and the unexplained weakness."

"And they haven't been able to find who's responsible?" she asked.

"No," the director said.

"When did they begin?"

Brad looked unhappy. "That's the reason I came to talk it over with you," he said. "From what the constable said, the attacks began about the time Barnabas Collins returned here."

She uttered a small gasp of protest. "Oh, no!"

"That's a fact," he said grimly.

Rita sat up very straight, pulling her dressing gown more tightly around her. "Barnabas couldn't possibly have anything to do with this," she said firmly.

"I'm not suggesting he has," Brad said. "I'm thinking of someone else. And what happened to you yesterday. What about that servant of his. That Joab."

He caught Rita unprepared. She hesitated, "I don't know. I can't imagine him being aggressive. He only attacked me because I intruded on the house which Barnabas had told him to guard."

"But he did attack you violently," Brad insisted.

"It really proves nothing."

"And Barnabas mentioned he had difficulty controlling him, because he is slightly retarded," the director added significantly.

Rita became annoyed. "Of course you can make it seem he is guilty if you're going to deliberately build up a case against him."

"Please, Rita!" Brad raised a hand. "Don't think I'm looking for trouble. It's the last thing on my mind."

"Well?"

"I'm just suspicious of that Joab. I didn't say anything to the police about what happened to you yesterday. For one thing, I didn't want them prying around here interfering with our shooting schedule. For another, I didn't want to put Barnabas on a spot, but I think you should discuss the attacks with him."

"I—I don't think Joab is guilty."

"But just on the chance," he urged.

"If you particularly want me to," she said.

Brad looked less unhappy. "Thanks. I don't want to stir up anything, but if any of our girls are molested again I'll have no choice. I can't allow a maniac to stalk the women in the company."

"I understand," she said in a dull voice.

"Please don't get upset about it, Rita," Brad pleaded. "And come down for the first shots as soon as you can. We're pretty nearly ready."

"I won't be long," she told him.

After he'd gone, she lingered listlessly over the breakfast plate for several minutes, doing nothing more than take tiny, thoughtful sips of the coffee. Her mind was in a furore. Suppose Joab was responsible? It would put poor Barnabas in a very difficult position. And in spite of the brave front she'd presented to Brad she wasn't at all certain but that Joab was the attacker.

Blanche bustled up to her. "Have some more of your breakfast, Miss Glenn. You have a long, difficult day ahead."

"I'm not hungry," Rita said.

"That man!" Blanche said, glaring over at the door. "Coming here with his wild stories to upset you."

Rita smiled wanly. "I'll be all right. I promise."

"All right!" the older woman fussed. "It's not what I'd call it, trying to do a long hard morning's work with no nourishment in your stomach."

Rita forced herself to eat a little more to placate the troubled woman and then changed into her costume to go downstairs. It was an early nineteenth-century dress and Blanche carefully placed a wig on her head to conform with the hair dress of the period. Then the older woman accompanied her downstairs, carrying along a small bag of make-up for last-minute touches.

Brad already had the crew ranged before the gaunt old tree with its spread of dead limbs. C. Stanton Shaw in long coat and tight breeches looked exactly like the bigoted small-town personage he was playing in the film. He was the only one appearing with her in this scene and he was waiting patiently to one side.

Brad greeted her with a smile. "All ready, Rita? You know where this scene begins?"

"Yes," she said. "I know the lines."

He came to stand close by her, concerned. "Are you sure you're all right? You're very pale."

"I'm fine," she assured him. "Let's begin."

It wasn't a long scene but it was a dramatic one with a great deal of tension between her and C. Stanton Shaw. The old character actor fairly hurled his abusive lines at her and she was forced to a rebuttal that took a great deal of energy. The dialogue between them was being filmed directly in front of the gaunt tree and Brad let the cameras roll through the complete scene without a cut.

When they'd finished he came over to them. "That was great as far as delivering the lines was concerned," he told them both. "But I think we can get a more interesting camera angle. We'll take a brief rest and begin it again." Rita was familiar with the director's methods. Brad was a tireless worker himself and expected everyone else to be. He had the scene repeated five times before he felt he had enough material recorded to make a satisfactory sequence. It took nearly all the day, and by the time they ended work around four in the afternoon Rita was exhausted enough to go upstairs at once for a short nap before dinner.

Brad went to the village that evening and she waited for Barnabas to come and call on her. By the time eight o'clock had arrived she began to be really on edge. She had been filling in time with a bridge game with Stanton Shaw and two of the older men on the technical crew. At last she grew so nervous she could no longer concentrate on the game and asked to be excused. David Billings took over her hand and the game went on while she moved over to the living room window and stared out into the darkness. Where could Barnabas be? Why hadn't he shown up?

She began to believe with Brad that Joab was the one involved in the attacks and Barnabas knew about it. Perhaps because of the incident which had happened the night before, Barnabas didn't dare to make an appearance, fearing that awkward questions might be asked. It had to be that. Otherwise, she was sure he wouldn't disappoint her.

At nine o'clock one of the chief electricians came in and she asked him if he'd seen any sign of Barnabas. "I know you must have met him since you've been here several days," she said.

"You mean the Englishman who lives in the old house," the electrician said with a smile on his broad face. "I was talking to him the other night when I was out there working. Very nice gentleman. He often goes into Collinsport for the evening. I think he drops by the Blue Whale."

"The tavern," she said.

"That's it. It's the only one in town unless you count the lounge in the hotel," the electrician said.

"Do you suppose he's gone to the Blue Whale tonight?" she asked.

He considered. "I wouldn't be surprised. Come to think of it, I haven't seen him or that queer servant of his around."

It was enough to make Rita decide to visit Collinsport. A few inquiries around among the staff and she found there was a car she could use, and shortly after nine she began the drive along the lonely side road that led to the main highway and the village of Collinsport.

Her hope was that she might locate Barnabas at the Blue Whale and have a chance to talk to him. She was anxious to warn him that Joab was being suspected of the attacks on women in the district and advise him to keep a closer rein on the man.

She met little traffic along the way but found parking space at a premium in the area of the brightly lighted Blue Whale. Feeling slightly embarrassed, she entered the crowded and noisy tavern alone and was at once conscious of a lot of attention being given her. At least some of the patrons were females and that helped, but there were still a lot of people staring at her.

She was trying to get up enough courage to approach the burly bartender and ask him if Barnabas had been there during the evening when she saw a familiar face glaring at her from the end of the bar. It was none other than the stocky Joab who stood there with a glass of beer in hand and a menacing look on his beard-stubbled face. At once she became panicky and was going to turn and hurry out of the tavern.

But as she wheeled around she ran straight into a smiling Brad Hilton, who studied her with surprise. "What in the world are you doing here?"

She sighed. "I came looking for Barnabas."

"He was here," Brad said. "But he left a little while ago. Come sit in a booth with me and I'll tell you about it." He guided her back down the narrow crowded tavern, She let him lead her somewhat unwillingly, feeling that her mission had been pointless.

Brad found them an empty booth and when they were seated across from each other over the drinks he'd ordered, he told her about his meeting with Barnabas. "He was here when I first arrived," Brad said. "And that ugly Joab was with him."

"Joab's still here," Rita said unhappily, glancing over her shoulder in the direction of the bar to verify her statement and glimpse the servant's stocky figure standing there.

"I had a chance to talk to Barnabas alone," Brad said. "And I warned him."

"What did he say?"

"Not much. But he did seem concerned. I think my mentioning it will do some good."

She stared down at the table unhappily. "I can't fathom Barnabas. He promised he'd come to the house tonight and he didn't."

"And so you drove in here? Where did you get the car?"

She offered him a wry smile. "The camera department."

"Good for them," the director said. "They were no match for your charm."

"I really had to get away from Collinwood for a while," she said earnestly.

"But being out alone in this area isn't all that safe with some kind of lunatic roaming around and attacking women."

"It has to be Joab, I guess," she said. "The more I think about it the more I'm sure you're right."

"I told Barnabas that and he made no comment," Brad said with a resigned sigh. "I told him if there was another incident in the company I'd raise plenty of trouble."

"The way that Joab looked at me just now sent chills through me," Rita said, shuddering again at the thought of Joab's look.

"That's another thing," Brad said. "I don't know that he should be served alcohol. He's dangerous enough when he's sober."

"If you talked as straight as you say to Barnabas, he'll likely keep him at the house in future," was Rita's prediction.

"Let's hope so," the director said. "I'm worried about you. You should be home in bed now. We have another busy day of shooting tomorrow. And there's a strong chance that Clifton Kerr will arrive on his boat."

She grimaced. "Something to look forward to."

Brad was frowning. "Do you think you'll be safe driving back to Collinwood alone?"

"Of course," she said. "It's only a short drive."

"But you'll have to walk to the house after you park the car," the director worried.

She smiled. "I'll park it directly in front of the door and then have one of the crew put it away for the night."

"I like the idea," Brad agreed. "I'll see you to the car now. That Joab may have his eye on you."

"Now you're really making me jittery," Rita said.

"I'd take you back myself," he said, "but I have to stop by the hotel and have a conference with the script editor and assistant director. It could be a long one. I have ideas for a couple of changes."

She smiled wanly as she got up. "After I've learned all the lines as they are written?"

Brad was on his feet at her side. "There won't be many line changes. It will mostly be the action shots. It seems that every hour I'm finding new settings at Collinwood. Do you know there's a wonderfully quaint old cemetery out back?"

"It doesn't surprise me," she said as they started walking out.

"A girl named Victoria Winters, who lives with the Collins family, told me about it before they all left for Vermont," Brad said. "After we ended work today I went out back and took a look at it for myself. It has to be in the film."

She sighed. "You and your penchant for quaint old scenes!"

"Keep your eyes straight ahead; we're passing something reasonably quaint," he told her, and as they eased on out into the street, he added, "You were right. That Joab glares at you as if he'd like to throttle you."

"Or leave his peculiar mark on my throat," she said, making a joke of it since it seemed the only thing to do. She was whistling in the dark and knew it, but better that than breaking down completely.

Brad saw her to the car and peered in the window as she started the engine. "Drive straight to Collinwood," he told her. "And don't stop for anything or anybody until you get there."

"Count on that," she told him.

She didn't feel very brave as she left the main highway for the deserted side road to Collinwood. She kept picturing the ugly face of Joab as he'd glared at her from the bar. It was unlikely that he had any means of following her, but it still made her fearful.

There was no fog tonight, but in spite of there being plenty of stars the night was dark. The beams of the headlights of the sedan rocked up and down as it bumped along the rough side road. But they cut a path through the night and showed up the numerous curves. She had been forced to curb the speed of the car because of her unfamiliarity with the road and the thick bushes on either side of it which cut down visibility.

Then as she rounded a curve she was suddenly presented with a dramatic and frightening spectacle. The sight of a young girl struggling in the grasp of a dark-clad man. The shock of it made Rita scream out in fear and apply her foot to the brakes in order not to run the battling pair down. The car jolted to a halt, and as the headlights brought the two into full focus she caught a full glimpse of the disheveled, dark-haired girl whom she didn't recognize. Then the man turned his startled gaze towards her as if dazed and blinded by the glare of the headlights.

She almost fainted, for it was the tormented face of Barnabas Collins she saw for that quick second. Then he swiftly turned and vanished into the bushes. The girl had already run on ahead somewhere out of range of the lights. The motor of Rita's car was still running and she conquered her feelings of shock and nausea to put her foot on the gas pedal and send the car shooting forward.

Nor did she let up in speed until she reached the front entrance of Collinwood. Two of the crew were standing talking on the steps. In a rather breathless fashion she hurried out of the car and gave the key to one of them, asking him to park it in its regular place. Then she went inside and rushed upstairs to her room.

Not until she had closed the door behind her and was on the fourposter bed did it fully hit her, and she burst into an uncontrollable sobbing that lasted for some time. She had been hit so hard emotionally she was not able to reason. And not until some of her shock drained off in tears was she able to face what she'd seen.

Barnabas Collins had been attacking the girl, and it took no great amount of deduction to guess that it had been Barnabas who'd waylaid the script girl the night before, and that he had also been responsible for the long series of incidents where young women had been assaulted on lonely roads at night since he'd arrived in the area. No wonder he had been reluctant to indict the brutish Joab since he knew himself to be the guilty one.

But what was behind it all? Had Barnabas become the victim of some madness? Rita couldn't associate the sedate, gentlemanly character of the man she'd known in London with the ruthless attacker of young women. And yet, it had to be.

Surely he was suffering from some sort of nervous breakdown brought on by overwork. Perhaps he tried to fight off this terrible weakness and yet succumbed to it. Because she loved Barnabas she was not going to allow what she had witnessed turn her from him in disgust. She must talk to him and ask him to be frank with her. They would find the reason for his compulsion and the cure for it.

It all began to fit together now like a weird jigsaw puzzle. His odd behavior and his reluctance to allow their romance to evolve into a marriage. His frantic pace of overwork and his dependence on the stolid Joab. He was behaving like a man on the edge of insanity and surely his actions in attacking these young women proved that he was badly in need of treatment.

At once she made up her mind to divulge what she had discovered to no one else until she had confronted Barnabas with it. What she did after that would depend on his reaction. Meanwhile, her dread secret would weigh heavily on her mind.

The test came the following morning when Brad Hilton confided in her that one of the village girls had been attacked the previous night. "It must have been about the time you were driving home," the director said. "You were lucky you missed it."

"Yes, I was," she said, using her talent as an actress not to betray her emotions.

"It had to be the same person who attacked the girl from our company," Brad said. "And we both saw Joab at the bar."

"Yes, we did."

"My guess is he left after we did and followed you on foot along the shore road. That is where the girl was assaulted."

Rita said, "I suppose it's another case of her not being able to tell who her attacker was?"

He nodded. "It always seems to be the same. The identical mark on their throats, as if they'd been bitten, and a completely foggy recollection of all that took place."

"Fear sometimes furnishes its own anesthesia," she pointed out.

The director looked grim. "It's too bad it does in these cases," he said. "It would help tremendously if just one of the girls could identify her attacker."

Rita went through the day's shooting in a state of tension, hardly able to wait for her working hours to end, and news that Clifton Kerr's palatial yacht had arrived and was docked at the estate wharf didn't even register with her. When the day's shooting ended, Brad, in deference to the temperamental Kerr, went down to the boat to see him. Kerr had made no attempt to leave it and mingle with the rest of the company.

Rita went to her room to change and freshen up. She felt more weary and frightened than she had in a long while, and Blanche noticed it in her. The buxom woman helped her into her dress for the evening and worried aloud.

"I say that Brad Hilton is working you too hard," Blanche declared angrily. "And now that Clifton Kerr is here it will be even worse."

"I'll be all right," Rita assured her.

"You don't look all right," Blanche worried. "You look like you might faint any minute and that's the truth."

Rita put up a brave front at dinner. Brad was full of talk about Kerr's boat and his comments about the script. "Kerr has a fabulous boat there," the tall man told her across the table. "But it hasn't improved his disposition. He isn't satisfied with the treatment we've given the story. He claims his part has been subordinated to yours."

She managed a smile. "Isn't that to be expected?"

C. Stanton Shaw raised his eyes from his plate. "From Kerr you get that every time."

David Billings ran a hand through his curly blond hair as he remarked, "And I suppose that horrible Dr. Moreno put in his two cents worth as well."

"Moreno stood right behind Kerr in his complaints about the script," Brad admitted. "But I did a lot of talking and I got him to accept it as it is for the time being anyway. No telling when he'll kick up, though."

Rita left them all discussing Kerr's attitude and the plans for the next day's location shooting. It was after sundown and she slipped out of Collinwood and made her way past the barns and through the field to the old house. As she hurried along she saw Barnabas emerge from the house. Apparently not seeing her, he turned and walked rapidly away. Rita increased her own pace to catch up with him. By the time she came close to him he was standing within the iron-railed confines of the Collins private cemetery. His back was to her and he wore his dark Inverness cape. He was sadly studying a worn white headstone with the name Josette barely discernible on it. Rita quietly made her way inside the cemetery and came to stand silently beside him.

He turned to stare at her with astonishment on his handsome, melancholy face. "You!" he said.

"Why should you be so surprised?" she asked.

He made no attempt to answer her. "Why have you followed me to this place?" he asked instead.

"Because you didn't come to meet me last night as you promised."

His black, deep-set eyes showed the torment that was surging within him. "I could not meet you," he said. "You mustn't expect to see me regularly while you are here. It's impossible for us to go on as we did before. It all ended for us in London."

"I refuse to believe that," Rita said defiantly.

He was staring at the worn headstone again. "You must," he said in a quiet voice. "Believe me I am as dead as the body that lies in that grave."

"What crazy thing are you saying?"

Barnabas turned to her again, his face shadowed with despair. "I am telling you the truth. I have no right to your love. In nearly all respects, I am a dead man."

"Don't talk that way," she said, alarmed. "I saw you last night. I know it was you who attacked that girl. And who attacked the others as well. I realize you are ill and I want to help see that you are cured."

"So you did recognize me," he said softly.

"Yes."

She was suddenly aware of how isolated they were here, and that if he were truly mad, as he sounded he might be, he could easily murder her here before anyone could arrive to her rescue. She had deliberately put herself in a terribly dangerous position. Yet, she had done it because she loved Barnabas and believed in him. So she would not let her fear govern her now.

"It's all part of it," he said in a strained voice. "Those girls mean nothing to me. They serve a purpose. Nothing more. How can I explain it to you? Make you understand?"

Rita was staring up into his handsome face, her eyes filled with sympathy. "You have to share it with someone. You've borne it too long as it is. You must tell me the truth."

"So it's the truth you want?" he said with a bitter smile. "All right, you shall have it. The truth is, I've been dead more than a century!"

CHAPTER 5

They stood there, two forlorn figures in the ancient cemetery, while he related the story of his past. Rita listened with a rapt, stricken look on her lovely face as he described the romance between himself and Josette on that distant day. Then he brought Angelique into the account and mentioned her jealousy and her knowledge of voodoo brought from the West Indies. Of her placing the curse on him so that he lost Josette to become a vampire, one of the living dead!

Barnabas's handsome face reflected his inward torture as he touched a hand to her arm and said, "You are the first great love of my life since that long ago day. And I have had to deny you because of what I have become."

Rita glanced down at his hand and saw that while she had not noticed it before it had a clawlike appearance. The hair on the back of his hand was coarse and heavy and the fingers were slim and of the color of clay. She gave an involuntary shudder.

"Already you fear me," he said in a tone of great sadness.

"No!" she protested, but she had turned away so as not to look at him.

"I have tried to keep the truth from you," he went on bitterly. "But last night you saw me. I have had to attack those girls.

I need their blood to survive. It is a thirst too strong for me to battle. But I swear I have done none of them any other harm."

"How long has this been going on?" she asked, still avoiding his eyes.

"For more than a century," he said. "Much longer than you can imagine. Nor can you have any idea of my weariness. My desire to age and die in a normal fashion."

She turned to him with horror-stricken eyes. "Is there no hope?"

"Through the decades I have traveled from country to country, consulted with every authority in the medical field," he said. "No one has been able to help me."

Rita took a few steps away from him and leaned weakly against a weathered tombstone, closing her eyes and attempting to make some sense of what the dignified Britisher had told her. She wasn't at all sure but what she'd have preferred him to be some sort of madman or criminal to the macabre creature he claimed to be.

It was almost impossible to believe. She had given her heart to a man who had first lived at the beginning of another century. Whose portrait painted a hundred years ago hung in the hall of Collinwood. So Barnabas was not really an Englishman but an American who had lived in the old country so long he had taken on British ways.

She felt that he was reaching out to her for understanding and that she must not deny him it. There could be little doubt that she was one of the few people who knew his secret.

Her back to him, and still leaning on the tombstone, she asked, "Does Joab know?"

"He is the only one besides you who does," Barnabas said. "I have had to hire and train trustworthy servants down through the years. That is why I hired an eccentric deaf-mute. He cannot easily communicate what he knows to others, and because I have been good to him he is fiercely loyal to me."

She touched a hand to her forehead. "It's such a fantastic story!"

Barnabas spoke from close behind her. "If you'd rather not believe it, just try to forget it. And forget about me as well."

Now she wheeled around to him with an earnest expression on her pretty face. "Don't talk that way, Barnabas! Whatever this curse is, I still love you."

His melancholy, high-cheekboned face became gentle. "If any words could break the spell, those would."

"There must be something we can do," she insisted. "You can't go on as you are. Eventually the police will catch up with you and you'll be in serious trouble."

His expression showed great weariness. "Don't think it hasn't happened before," he said. "When the uproar becomes too great I vanish and move on to another place."

"You can't go on being a lonely wanderer all your life," she said.

He took her hand in his and offered her a faint, bitter smile. "I know you would change things if it was in your power, but it isn't."

"Don't be so sure," she said. "I don't give up easily."

A raven came close over their heads, flapping its wings and uttering a melancholy cry. Rita became aware that dusk was well-advanced and the eerie call of the great black bird heightened the gloom of their surroundings. She stared at the rows of tombstones, some broken, others toppling, some weathered but in otherwise good condition. And she knew that these were the markers of people who were contemporaries of the man beside her. Had it not been for the curse put upon him Barnabas would be a grinning skull and scattered bones in one of those lonely graves.

"I think we should leave here," he said, as if he understood her thoughts.

She nodded, and as darkness came they walked slowly back up the hill to the old house. In the far distance she could hear the pounding of the waves and smell the salty tang in the air, but she was barely conscious of her surroundings, so tumultuous were her thoughts.

When they reached the old house Barnabas halted. "Before you go I think you should see where and how I spend my days."

There was something almost sinister in his voice that made her stare at him in fear, but she said, "If you wish."

"Come with me into the house," he said in a low voice. Inside he lit a candle and then led her to the cellar stairway. She followed him hesitantly into its dank depths and then along a narrow dark corridor. Barnabas held the candle aloft and its flame fluttered as they moved forward, throwing a soft reflection on his handsome face with its deep-set eyes.

Finally they came to a closed door. He glanced at her to see that she was still close behind him and then he lifted the latch on the door and thrust it open to reveal a drab, stone-walled room. It's only furnishings were a coffin on a stand with candelabra at top and bottom of it.

Barnabas moved near the coffin and turned to say, "My resting place during the daylight hours."

"Oh, no!" she protested, staring into the empty casket with the impression on the satin pillow where a head must have rested.

"It is part of the curse," Barnabas said. "I spend my days

here and Joab guards the house to be sure that no one discovers me."

She stared at him. "That is why he is so belligerent."

"He has served me well. It will be bad for me when age advances on him and I have to seek a substitute."

Rita lifted her head defiantly. "You'll not have to worry about that. You'll somehow be cured before then."

He stood there holding the candle to give a soft glow of light in the funeral chamber. "I wish I could believe that," he said.

And then a sudden thought struck her. "There is a doctor here at Collinwood now who might be able to help you."

"You must be joking," Barnabas said disbelieving.

"I'm not!" she insisted. "The man I speak of is a specialist in African diseases. He cured Clifton Kerr when no one else could. He arrived here today with Kerr. He's on the yacht docked at the estate wharf."

"I doubt if he could do anything," Barnabas said.

"I think differently," Rita told him. "His name is Dr. Moreno. He's not a very pleasant person, but he does have knowledge not shared by some of our regular doctors. I think there's a good chance he might be able to help you. And I wouldn't mind approaching him on your behalf."

Barnabas showed alarm. "No. I can't ask you to do that."

"I don't mind," she said. "I'll arrange for you to meet."

"I can't trust my secret with him," Barnabas protested. "Don't you understand?"

"I'll make the first contact," she promised. "I'll fix it so you can talk to him without being afraid."

"Rita, I thank you for what you want to do. I love you for it. But I daren't let you involve yourself."

She looked up at him with gentle eyes. "Silly! I am involved already. I love you."

The handsome face in the flickering light of the candle revealed fear and concern. "Then you are in danger. The curse is upon any who love me as well."

"I don't mind risking Angelique's curse," she said firmly. "And I can't ask it of you!"

"You're not asking it of me," Rita assured him. "I'm doing this on my own. I'll have some news for you tomorrow night. I'll come here to the house to meet you." She gave him a meaningful look. "And until then, please take care."

Barnabas turned away. "I shouldn't have told you."

"After last night you had no choice," she reminded him. "Now that I fully understand I can do something for you. I'm sure this Dr. Moreno has met up with voodoo and the illness caused by it before."

"But you said he wasn't a pleasant person," Barnabas reminded her.

"Nor is he," she said. "But we can put up with that to benefit from his talents. Don't you agree?"

Barnabas sighed. "What can I say? I know you're going ahead with whatever you have in mind anyway. Just don't be too let down when your plan fails."

"It isn't going to fail," she said. "It mustn't."

He saw her safely back upstairs and then walked as far as the entrance to Collinwood with her. The clutter of trucks and equipment seemed to belong to another world now, for Rita was so acutely sensitive to Barnabas's plight and his relationship with the ancient mansion.

"You were born here on the estate," she said, staring up at him as they stood on steps in the darkness.

"I roamed these hills and woods as a boy," he admitted, the sound of the surf underlining his words.

"One day we will marry here," Rita said softly. "When you have become a normal man again."

Barnabas smiled sadly down at her. "It is a beautiful dream even if it is an impossible one."

"You'll see!" she promised and she leaned forward for him to kiss her before they parted.

When his lips touched hers now she understood the coldness, and she no longer let it frighten her. If she truly loved Barnabas she must love him as he was.

She went inside and Brad Hilton was standing in the outer hallway just below the portrait with a knowing expression on his sensitive, battered face. "My second sight is at work again," he said. "I sense trouble for you and Barnabas Collins."

Rita looked startled. "I've just left him."

"I guessed that," the director said. "You've been awfully jumpy since seeing him again. Is he good for you?"

"Of course he is."

"It doesn't seem so," Brad said. "He's a strange person. He gives me the feeling that he belongs to another age. That he isn't of our time at all."

Rita bridled. "Are you criticizing his manners and reserve?"

The director raised his eyebrows. "Perhaps. But I doubt it. I think there is a certain air about him that's not of our day. Haven't you noticed it?"

Rita was determined not to reveal Barnabas's secret to Brad, even though she knew he was her friend and concerned about her. She said, "I find Barnabas very relaxing. I think it's the adjustment to the conditions here that has made me nervous."

"Steel yourself," Brad warned her. "We're going to do some scenes with Clifton Kerr on the lawn tomorrow. And you'll need all your strength and patience."

She smiled. "I'll keep that in mind," she promised, and she went on up the broad stairway.

Her mind was such a turmoil of thoughts she found it hard to get to sleep, and when sleep did come at last it brought some disconcerting dreams. She was in that gloomy cellar room and standing over Barnabas's coffin. He was in the casket with eyes closed and waxen hands folded on his breast as if in actual death. As she stared at him in panic a single drop of blood oozed from the corner of his heavy lips. The drop of blood became bigger until it ran in a trickle across his face. The sight of it made her scream!

The scream woke her and she sat up in bed. The room was in darkness and all at once she felt that chilling presence again. And the scent of wild violets filled the air around her, the sweet scent stifling her! She groped her way from the bed and started for the door without robe or slippers in a rush to call Blanche and ask for her company. And just as she reached the door she was sure she heard soft female laughter from the darkness behind her.

She knocked on the door of Blanche's room and she was still trembling when the buxom woman answered it. She explained she'd had a nightmare and asked Blanche to keep her company for a while. The stout woman was concerned and returned to the room with her and gave her a sleeping pill.

The sleeping pill gave Rita undisturbed rest for the balance of the night. She awoke the following morning feeling drowsy and with her mind in a somewhat confused state. It was not until she had coffee that she began to place the events of the night in focus. She was sure that when she'd awakened from her nightmare she'd been visited by that mocking feminine ghost again. And she had an idea it was Angelique who was returning to torment her. Angelique in a strange battle with her for Barnabas's soul. He had mentioned the violet perfume and spoke of it reminding him of someone in his past.

But she was forced to put aside these speculations and begin the day's work. When she was in costume she went downstairs and found the rest of the company waiting for her to do the several scenes on the lawn.

Of course Clifton Kerr was the most prominent of the group, and he made a show of being pleased to see her. He came over to greet her looking impressive in his century-old costume. He was a thin, black-haired man with a long, sensitive face of the romantic type to make hearts flutter when it flashed on the movie screens of the world. Although he was only of medium height his bearing made him seem taller.

Now he kissed Rita properly on the cheek and said, "Darling, how well you look! Maine must agree with you."

"I'm not sure about that," she said with a small smile in return. "I haven't been here long enough yet."

"You should have come down to the boat last night," he reproved her.

"I thought you'd want to rest."

The leading man grimaced. "Fat chance with most of the company there lapping up my liquor. But we'll change all that. I'm making rules. Only certain people to come on board. We'll have plenty of time for ourselves before the shooting is finished."

Brad joined them with a genial smile. "I'm glad to find you in a friendly mood," he said. "You begin in this film as lovers even though you do come to hate each other later."

"I call it a stupid script," the leading man said with a frown. "And Moreno agrees."

"Let's at least try it in this version," Brad argued. "If it doesn't work out we'll get some rewrites."

Kerr gave Rita a despairing look. "You see how it is, Darling. You simply can't reason with them."

Since it was in this atmosphere the work on the scenes began it was not surprising that the results were less than satisfactory. Brad kept groaning and asking them to try sections again while he rearranged cameras and sound-booms. Clifton Kerr overacted by Rita's standards and did all he could to hog every scene. She curbed her desire to reprove him and played her part quietly, as it was written.

At noon the sun vanished and before lunch was over it had begun to shower. This meant the end of work for the day. Kerr left to go back to the boat after giving Rita an invitation to come down and visit him anytime. She gladly accepted the invitation since she wanted to talk to Dr. Moreno, who had not appeared on the set. She was delighted that the rain had come and soon after lunch she donned raincoat and hat and started down to the boat.

The big yacht overwhelmed the wharf down the beach from Collinwood. A sailor was on guard and stood aside politely when she informed him who she was. She asked where she might find Dr. Moreno and he directed her toward a cabin door at the bow.

She walked the length of the trim white boat noting that the rain was not letting up and the clouds overhead were still black and forbidding. They would see no sun until tomorrow.

Entering the cabin she came face to face with the rather sinister Dr. Moreno, who must have seen her approaching. He was wearing a gray suit and black sunglasses even though the day was dark. He had the dusky skin of a Southern European and the demonic features of a minor Satan.

"This is a nice surprise," he said in his urbane fashion. "But I'm afraid Clifton is having an afternoon nap, and I hesitate to wake him to let him know you're here."

"Please don't," she begged. "I came to see you."

"Indeed," Dr. Moreno said, the swarthy face showing surprise, although the dark glasses concealed any expression in his eyes.

"I suppose you think that's strange," she said.

Dr. Moreno smiled coldly. "Few of Clifton's associates bother making my acquaintance or cultivating my friendship. I often feel that I am a necessary but unfortunate presence."

"You shouldn't," she objected, studying the luxurious furnishings of the good-sized cabin.

He waved to a divan built into the wall and upholstered in a rich green. "Won't you please sit down since we're going to talk."

"Thank you," she said and sat primly.

Dr. Moreno sank into an easy chair with his hands grasping its arms as he directed the dark glasses at her. She had the feeling that behind their facade his shrewd eyes were giving her a penetrating glance.

"So you have come to see me," he said.

"Yes."

The doctor smiled that cold smile again. "I find that flattering if a little unusual. Did Brad send you with some complaint? Am I to give Clifton a lecture? Did he misbehave on the set today?"

"Nothing like that," she told the dark-skinned man.

"I'm more interested than ever," he said. "Then what brings you here?"

"I want to seek your professional advice."

He gave her a mocking glance. "You don't look as if you require medical aid."

"Not for myself," she said. "But for a friend."

"Indeed," Moreno said without expression. "Of course you know I'm devoting my full time to Clifton these days. I'm no longer in active medical practice."

"I realize that," Rita agreed. "But I hoped you might make an exception for me. For my friend."

The swarthy man regarded her slyly. "You must think a great deal of this friend."

"I do," she said. "He is very close to me."

"A man!" Dr. Moreno looked wise. "You hadn't made that

clear until now. And so you wish me to see this fellow. What ails him?"

She hesitated. "It is not an easy disease to describe," she said at last.

"I see," Dr. Moreno said. "A difficult case."

"Yes. But with your background in African diseases I'm sure you'll be able to suggest treatment."

"There must first be a diagnosis," he reminded her in his mocking way.

She blushed. "I realize that, but I don't think you'll find his condition difficult to decide about. I told him about the wonders you have worked for Clifton—that he wasn't even able to work until you took him under your care."

"I sometimes wonder if it was worth it," Dr. Moreno said with a hint of disgust. "I gave up leading a very promising sect to restore his health. It often seems to me that he isn't properly grateful."

"I'm sure he is."

Moreno smiled coldly. "I'm well paid. That's even better than gratitude. And may I take this opportunity to remind you that should I see your friend, my fees will be high."

"The presents no problem," she said.

"I wanted it clearly understood," Dr. Moreno stated, "that if I see this man I'll only be doing it as a favor to you."

"And I'll appreciate it," she said.

"Enough to protect Clifton's interests in this film?" the swarthy doctor wanted to know. "He intends to demand script changes, will you back him up in this?"

She hesitated. "I will if there's a good reason."

"If I consent to treat your friend you'll do it when and as I dictate it," Dr. Moreno said in a hard voice. "I make Clifton's important decisions for him, as you must know." Rita was desperate. She had no choice but to bargain with the unscrupulous man who had her co-star in his power and was apparently working hard to get her in the same position.

She said, "I'll be cooperative."

"That's better," he snapped, giving her a look of scorn. He gave her the feeling he possessed a deep inferiority complex and his only way of compensating was to hate people, to hold power over them and demean them. She disliked placing herself in a position where she might owe him favors, but there was Barnabas to be considered. That was the most important problem in her life at the moment.

She hesitated. "I'd like to bring him here to see you this evening, if that is all right."

Dr. Moreno smiled nastily. "You make it sound very urgent."

"It is."

"What sort of sickness did you say it was?"

Rita felt her cheeks crimson. "I didn't say, but I believe it will fall in your specialty. It has to do with voodoo. An African type of illness."

"Indeed?" Moreno said. "Now you interest me. What is your friend's name?"

She disliked revealing it but knew it could not be held back. She said, "His name is Barnabas Collins. He lives in the old house here. I knew him in London."

"One of the Collins family," the doctor said. "I understood they had vacated the estate to us for the duration of the film."

"All but Barnabas," she said. "He is not living in the main house."

The doctor looked thoughtful. "Barnabas Collins," he said. "The name has a familiar ring to it."

"I doubt that you know him," she said. "But I would like to bring him here to consult with you tonight."

The eyes behind the dark glasses regarded her. "You will be coming with him."

"I think it would be best. He is a rather sensitive person," she said. "It will not be easy for him."

"I see," Dr. Moreno said. "Very well. You may come here to this cabin at nine. Clifton will be entertaining some friends, but he will use the main cabin."

"Thank you," she said, rising. "I won't keep you any longer."

He offered her an oily smile. "But I always enjoy your company, Rita. I consider you one of the screen's loveliest women, and you have a great talent. But you should have a better agent. Someone like me."

Rita couldn't hide her embarrassment. She definitely disliked the dark man but she couldn't show it now. She looked down, saying, "I'm sorry. I'm already signed with an agency for a long contract."

The man with the dark glasses took her arm familiarly as he led her to the cabin door. "These contracts can be easily broken," he assured her. "I know all about it. Think it over. Your present contract presents no problem. I can handle that."

"Thanks," she said hurriedly, anxious to get away from him. "I'll come with Mr. Collins at nine."

"Nine will be excellent," Dr. Moreno said. "And don't mention what I said about the script to Brad. I want to spring it on him at exactly the right moment without warning. Until then, say nothing. Of course, I'll count on your lining up with Clifton and me when I offer an ultimatum."

"Yes," she said in a small voice.

"Good," Dr. Moreno said with another of his unpleasant smiles. "I'll tell Clifton that you were here and that we have you on our side. It will make him very happy." She left the boat and hurried up the path to Collinwood. It was still showering and she didn't want to get too wet. She was also as anxious to get as much distance between herself and the boat as she could. The meeting with the sinister Dr. Moreno could not have been more unpleasant. And she already felt she had besmirched herself to gain his good will and have him agree to treat Barnabas.

How much more demanding would the unscrupulous doctor be when he learned the full truth about the illness from which Barnabas suffered? Would he make use of the information to blackmail her even further. And she worried that perhaps Barnabas was right, that her visit to the doctor on his behalf had been a mistake. She suddenly could not imagine a charlatan like Moreno being capable of helping Barnabas where so many others had failed.

But Moreno had been successful with Clifton Kerr when he was in dire physical straits. She had heard all the stories of the star's being unable to work or even show himself in the sunlight. Yet Dr. Moreno had cured his fever and gradually restored his health to the point of normalcy. Surely it was possible he could at least help Barnabas.

That was her gamble, and it appeared that Moreno intended to make her pay well in cash and favors for seeing Barnabas and giving his opinion of him. She was filled with fear and revulsion, but she knew she'd gone so far that there was no turning back.

As she entered the house she found Brad in discussion with C. Stanton Shaw. Brad left Shaw to come over to greet her with a solemn expression.

"You shouldn't be out walking in the rain," he said.

"I'm sorry," she murmured, feeling guilty. Knowing that only minutes ago she had agreed to enter into a conspiracy against the director.

He studied her intently. "You know, I have a hunch about you," he said. "My second sight is bothering me again, and I still see nothing but trouble for you and that Barnabas."

CHAPTER 6

By seven thirty the showers had ended and the fog had rolled in again. The foghorn on Collinsport Point began its steady, melancholy dirge and an accompanying depression settled on the houseful of players at Collinwood. Brad Hilton had gone into the village with the assistant director to look at some rushes of the day's shooting. And Rita, her nerves on edge as she waited to go meet Barnabas for their appointment with Dr. Moreno, found herself in the company of Stanton Shaw.

They had gone into the high-ceilinged living room together after dinner and sat facing each other in high-backed chairs near the window overlooking the ocean. The crystal chandelier overhead had been turned on, but it inadequately lightened the big room, and the old actor's face was somewhat in shadow as she sat across from him.

Resting his elbows on the chair arm he clasped his hands and gave her a significant look. "Have you noticed the brooding atmosphere of this old place?" he asked in his somewhat harsh voice.

Rita hesitated. "I suppose its age does impress me," she said.

"I mean more than that," Shaw persisted. "I believe Brad chose this place because it has an atmosphere of tragedy about it. He hoped to capture it in the film. And he may well do it."

"The location by the sea is isolated and impressive," she agreed, not exactly sure where the old man might be leading the conversation.

He eyed her shrewdly. "And the older house. The one where that Britisher lives. It must be interesting. I hear it dates back far beyond this one."

"Yes," she said carefully. "It does."

"I'd like to have a look at it one day," the old man said, his gaze fixed on her. "I understand you're a friend of this Barnabas Collins."

"I knew him when I was on the stage in London."

"Ah, yes," said Shaw. "You did begin your career in London. That accounts for your excellent training. I should like to meet your friend Barnabas Collins and have a look at that old house."

"I'll speak to him about it," Rita said with caution. "No doubt it can be arranged before we leave."

"I hope so," the old actor said, hunching in his chair and glaring out the window at the thickening fog. "I must say the weather hasn't favored us since we've begun work. It will have to be better than this if we're to keep on schedule."

"The nights and early mornings are often foggy when the days are clear and sunny," she said. "We can hope it will be better tomorrow."

The bald, wizened man nodded. "I think you're doing an excellent piece of acting in your role, but I can't say I enjoyed the way Clifton Kerr chewed scenery this morning. There is overacting and there is overacting! He played like an amateur."

"Perhaps he was tense. His first day on the set."

"With his experience that's a poor excuse," the character actor said disgustedly. "The truth is, he is a small talent and he's bent on stealing the glory from you in this film. I don't like the fellow. And I find the relationship between him and that slimy Dr. Moreno disgraceful."

Rita found herself in a strange predicament. While she agreed with the old man in all respects she could not declare herself because of her dependence on Moreno to help Barnabas. It was placing her in a difficult spot.

"I believe Dr. Moreno brought him back to health," she said finally.

The old man scowled. "There's a mystery about that, as well. I'd call Moreno a charlatan of the worst type. And yet Kerr was near death before Moreno treated him. I sometimes wonder if it wasn't a natural improvement Kerr had and that wily doctor took the credit for it."

"I hardly think so," Rita said, worried at the possibility.

"And the way Moreno has taken over his career," Shaw said with indignation. "He had full control of Kerr's earnings and you can bet he siphons off a good share for himself. And worse than that, he's always interfering on the set. He'll be doing that soon with Brad Hilton. You wait and see!"

Rita glanced away, hoping the old man would not notice the change in her expression, for she already knew tha Moreno was going to tackle Hilton about making changes in the script. And he was using blackmail of sorts to ensure that she went along with him even though she would be undermining her own role in the film by doing so.

In a small voice she said. "I realize the doctor has a difficult personality."

"The man's a crook!" Shaw snorted. "I ignore him whenever I can, and I think Brad will know how to deal with him. We're fortunate in having such a fine director. He'll not be intimidated by the likes of Moreno!"

Rita had heard enough on the subject. A few minutes later she excused herself on the basis of her going to meel Barnabas and left Shaw sitting alone in the shadowed room. She put on her coat and made her way out of the house and around to the back.

Her mind was in a turmoil with the conversation which had just ended. If Shaw should be right, she was making a grave error in taking Barnabas to Moreno. But the situation was so desperate she was forced to clutch at an; straw. Even though Moreno was surely a charlatan it was possible he possessed some knowledge of primitive African medicine that would come in useful in treating Barnabas.

She had to believe that or she would give way to complete despair. She was trembling slightly as she passed the outbuildings wreathed in the thick fog and headed for the old house. Not a light was showing and she thought of Barnabas living there in that dank atmosphere with no companion except the weird Joab. That a charming, sensitive person like Barnabas should be doomed to such an existence was shocking. She felt an intense hatred for the long-dead Angelique who had cruelly condemned him to this life.

When she got to the entrance of the older house the door was closed and there was no sign of Barnabas. It was getting late and he should have been expecting her. She began to have uneasy feelings that he might have changed his mind and decided against seeing Dr. Moreno. That could be a true disaster.

Raising a slim hand she used the heavy brass door knocker. It was a long moment before the door was slowly opened and the thick, brutish features of Joab peered out at her from the shadows.

The small reddish eyes fixed on her with a malevolence which made her shudder, and the beard-stubbled face wore an expression of hatred. He made no motion to let her enter the house or go inform Barnabas she had arrived.

Summoning all her courage, she said, "I've come to visit your master. Where is he?"

Joab continued to gaze at her in the same menacing fashion and then he uttered a weird snarling sound and slammed the door in her face. She stood there on the steps frustrated and stunned.

What had gone wrong? Where was Barnabas? It would soon be time to leave if they were going to keep their appointment with the doctor. She couldn't understand it. And she knew that there was no use knocking on the door again and trying to reason further with Joab. He hated her because of her influence on Barnabas and he was in no way prepared to be of help.

And then she had a sudden inspiration. Barnabas must have already left the somber surroundings of the old house. He probably had wanted to be alone to consider the move he was about to make. And if this should be the case where would he have gone? She turned on the steps and stared off into the gray mist. The most likely place was the cemetery where she had found him the night before. It apparently was a place where he often went to meditate.

Having come to this decision she quickly went down the steps and started through the field that led down the hill to the cemetery. The cold was penetrating and she clutched the tweed coat to her. She'd not gone more than fifty yards when she saw a cloaked figure coming up the hill. As the figure emerged from the fog she recognized Barnabas.

As they met she said, "I was frantic about you. I went to the house and Joab behaved badly, slamming the door in my face."

His face shadowed. "I'm sorry. Joab is overprotective of me, and he suspects you will bring me harm."

She touched his arm gently and looked up into the weary face. "You know I would never do that!"

Barnabas nodded. "Not purposely."

"Not at all."

He gave her a penetrating look with his deep-set piercing eyes. "I have been doing a great deal of thinking," he said. "And I don't feel it would be wise for me to see this Moreno. It's ridiculous to expect him to be able to help me."

"I disagree," she said. "I've already prepared him for your visit. And he seemed interested." She refrained from telling him her doubts about Moreno or the other unpleasant facts of her interview with him. It would only take that to make him refuse to go to the boat at all.

Barnabas remained reluctant as he stood there in the deserted field. "From all I've gathered, this Moreno is an unscrupulous person," he said. "Once I've exposed myself to him I could be placing both myself and you in a position to be blackmailed."

She was startled to hear that he had come to this conclusion on his own. But then she knew she shouldn't be. Barnabas was an intelligent man and Moreno had been fairly obvious in his behavior.

She said, "I don't care about his character as a man. If he has the ability as a doctor to save you then it's worth it."

Barnabas sighed. "I had made up my mind against it."

"Please," she begged. "For me. And for what it can mean to us and our love."

Barnabas gave her a fond look. Then he took her in his arms and their lips met. Still holding her close to him, he said in a low resigned voice, "Very well. For what might be."

They began the walk to the wharf. He was silent all the way and she knew he was far from happy about the decision he'd made. He really had no hope Dr. Moreno could cure him and was doing it simply to satisfy her.

For her part she felt guilty that she had not fully divulged the kind of person Moreno was to him, but he would soon know that for himself. And she was also filled with misgivings that their mission would be a failure.

Barnabas took her arm to help her down the rocky path that led to the beach and the wharf. Above, hovering gulls mewed in the damp fog, the waves continued their relentless wash on the shore, and the far-distant foghorn completed the lonely symphony. As they reached the wharf and neared the yacht they saw that cabins both fore and aft had lights. From the main cabin there came the sound of loud recorded music and the slightly drunken laughter of mixed company, and it was evident that Clifton Kerr was having the party Dr. Moreno had mentioned. In a way she was grateful for this, since it would keep him occupied and they would have privacy for their interview with the doctor.

Dr. Moreno opened the door of the forward cabin to their knock. He was alone and waiting for them. He wore a white dinner jacket and black tie and he had on his dark glasses as usual, but he greeted them in a manner that was affable for him.

"I'm glad you came," he said, standing back for them to enter. "I was worried that something might have prevented you from getting here."

"I was late meeting Mr. Collins," Rita alibied.

Dr. Moreno closed the door after them and waved them to sit on the green divan. "Please, make yourselves comfortable," he invited them.

Barnabas gave her a knowing look and they moved towards the divan. She turned to the doctor and said, "Forgive me, I didn't introduce you. This is Barnabas Collins, Dr. Lee Moreno."

Dr. Moreno smiled and shook Barnabas's hand, holding it for just a moment longer than she would have expected. And whether it was imagination or not she thought a strange look had come to the doctor's face.

After they were seated he stood before them with a glass in hand. "Can I get you a drink?" he asked.

Barnabas was seated in a very straight, formal fashion. "No," he said.

"Not for me either," Rita said. Then, with a glance at Barnabas, she added, "I think it's important we get right down to what we came for."

Dr. Moreno nodded silently. Then he settled himself in a swivel easy chair opposite them and gave his full attention to Barnabas. "Rita has been rather vague about your complaint," he said. "But I gather that it is African in origin and you have come to me because of my knowledge of African diseases."

Barnabas met his direct gaze. The deep-set eyes showed worry and he hesitated before explaining. "My trouble had its origin in the West Indies. But it is of a similar type."

"Of course," Dr. Moreno agreed. "Please go on."

Again Barnabas held back before he said with obvious difficulty, "It began a long while ago. It started with the bite of a bat-like creature. Since then I have not enjoyed normal health."

Dr. Moreno put down his glass and the eyes behind the dark glasses fixed on the unhappy Barnabas mockingly. "I can see that, Mr. Collins. Your condition is fairly clear to me. It has been from the moment we shook hands. You are a vampire, are you not?"

"I've not suggested that!" Barnabas exclaimed, rising to his feet.

Dr. Moreno smiled at him suavely. "No need for dramatics, Mr. Collins. I'm not shocked unless you are. You forget I'm fairly well acquainted with African medicines and voodoo."

Rita could keep silent no longer. "The important question is, can you help him?" she said, leaning forward.

"That we must consider," Moreno said in his oily manner. He waved to Barnabas. "Please sit down and relax, Mr. Collins. I dislike scenes."

Barnabas frowned and sat again. He said, "If you have any help to offer me let me hear about it. I haven't time for idle talk or games."

Moreno lolled in his chair and gave him a nasty smile. "On the contrary, Mr. Collins, you have a great deal of time. In fact I rather imagine anyone who has roamed the earth for more than a century must have lost all count of the days, even the years!"

"I have made no admissions," Barnabas reminded him.

"There has been no need for you to," Dr. Moreno said, his voice suddenly taking on a harder tone. "I have used my stay here to good advantage. Especially since Rita came to me about your case. I have done some research and I gather you are the original Barnabas Collins, born right here. And that it was you who suffered the curse of Angelique."

"Please do not go over all that," Rita begged. "Let us know if there is hope?"

Dr. Moreno turned to her calmly. "Before I can offer treatment or a cure I must complete my diagnosis. And the history of your friend is part of my diagnosis. In other words you are asking me to restore normalcy to a man who should have died a natural death a century and more ago."

"Please!" she begged. "Barnabas has suffered too much!"

"I'm familiar with his sufferings," Dr. Moreno said with his cynical smile. "As familiar as I am with the message of voodoo drums in the jungle night. I can imagine the ravages of thirst you must endure, Mr. Collins. A thirst for blood which you must have to sustain your peculiar state of life. And I'm sure the authorities would be interested to know of your case and the reason for the attacks on young girls in the vicinity these past weeks. And the meaning of the teeth-marks on their throats!"

Barnabas had risen again. He told her, "Let's get out of here!"

"Please, Barnabas!" she looked up at him imploringly.

"I meant no offense, Mr. Collins," the doctor said placatingly. "I just feel that all the facts should be understood between us."

"Say what you have to say quickly," Barnabas demanded glaring at him, his handsome face pale with anger.

Dr. Moreno nodded approvingly. "I like your spirit, Mr. Collins, It is most admirable in one in your desperate state. You are surely a brave man and I can see why Rita is so interested in you."

"I said to get on with it!" Barnabas told him.

There was a moment of silence in the small cabin. From a distance could be heard the sounds of the revelry in the other cabin. Then Dr. Moreno leaned forward and said quietly, "You have come to the right person, Mr. Collins. I can cure you."

It was so unexpected that it stunned both Barnabas and Rita into silence again. Barnabas sat down on the divan and gave her a troubled look, as if the news were too good to believe.

Barnabas said quietly, "I hope that is not merely idle talk,

Dr. Moreno."

"Do not worry. It isn't," the doctor said with assurance. "I did not waste my years in Africa. I studied under the most expert of the voodoo practitioners and I learned secrets known by no other white man. I can reverse the effect of the curse and make you a normal man. You will know the complete freedom of action of any other human being and in due time you will age and die. That is part of it."

Barnabas said, "That is what I want. A normal life with the usual ending."

"Then you can have it," Dr. Moreno said. "Under my treatment your condition will improve immediately. There will be no long delays. No endless waiting. You need not worry about my making promises I cannot keep. Within hours after I have begun to treat you it will be possible for you to walk in the daylight."

"Isn't that wonderful news, Barnabas?" Rita said, turning to Barnabas, her face bright with happiness.

Barnabas still showed disbelief. "You promise too much," he told the doctor in a low voice.

Dr. Moreno offered one of his mocking smiles again. "You mean there must be a catch in it? Well, there is. I'll require certain professional cooperation from Rita concerning this film we're making. She has agreed to help me, so that presents no problem. But there is also the question of fees. Mine are going to be rather expensive, Mr. Collins."

"How expensive?" Barnabas asked, his deep-set eyes never leaving the doctor's face.

"You will require an injection of a serum I have perfected," Dr. Moreno said. "And you will need it every forty-eight hours. Otherwise your condition will at once begin to deteriorate and you will revert to your present state. As long as you continue to enjoy the benefits of my serum you will have a perfectly normal life with a normal appetite and the capacity for all aspects of living. Including a normal romance." He glanced at Rita with a kind of leer as he said this.

Barnabas took a deep breath. "I require the injections every two days. What will you charge for each injection?"

"Two hundred dollars each injection, Mr. Collins," the doctor said firmly. "And I consider that most reasonable considering you will no longer suffer from your peculiar thirst. That you need not sleep in a casket by day and roam the lanes by night searching for the blood from tender throats!"

"Stop!" Barnabas said angrily. "Regardless of your powers I warn you I will listen to only so much."

Dr. Moreno spread his hands in a gesture of resignation.

"Forgive me, Mr. Collins. I only wanted to make it plain I'm offering you a rare bargain."

"You must be joking!" Rita said angrily. "It would take a movie star's earnings to pay that kind of money."

"Exactly," the doctor said. "Are you willing to give Mr. Collins a normal life, Rita? You have the money."

"No need of that," Barnabas spoke up. "I can well afford your treatments. I was left a sizable fortune a century and a half ago. It has continually increased with interest through the years until I now have a comfortable fortune. I can pay for the treatments, Dr. Moreno. I just ask you to prove that they will work."

"That can easily be settled," the doctor said in his oily manner. "You shall get the first treatment now. And it shall be free. Within twelve hours you will be back to normal. Before tomorrow noon you'll walk in the sunshine. After that, the injections will be on the cash basis which I mentioned."

"I agree," Barnabas said.

"Excellent," Dr. Moreno told him, getting to his feet. "Now, if you will just bare your right arm, Mr. Collins, I'll prepare the injection."

Rita helped Barnabas off with his cape and the dark suit coat underneath. Then he slowly rolled up his shirt sleeve to reveal his muscular, hairy arm. He gave her a what-can-we-lose look. She returned a smile of encouragement, for it was true they had nothing to lose and everything to gain. If the doctor's injection didn't work there would be no need to pay him for succeeding ones.

Dr. Moreno had unlocked a drawer of his desk and taken out a case with a hypodermic needle and a glass tube of thick, yellowish liquid. He proceeded to ready the hypodermic and fill it with the odd-looking substance. Rita watched him with anxious eyes, feeling that he had expected things to turn out exactly as they had and prepared himself for the situation.

The doctor came over to Barnabas. "This is going to be more painful than an ordinary injection, Mr. Collins," he warned him. "Both the sting of the needle and the reaction of the serum will cause you some discomfort. But only this initial time. The succeeding ones will be painless."

Rita turned away for a moment, and when she looked at Barnabas again he'd received the injection and the sallow tone of his handsome face had changed to an almost beet-red. He was obviously in intense pain.

"Are you all right?" she asked.

He nodded. But he hesitated in rolling down his shirt sleeve and putting on his coat. She knew that the hurt he was experiencing must be intense, and when she helped roll down the sleeve she winced at the sight of his puffed, angry arm. She assisted him with his coats as well.

Dr. Moreno studied him. "You have a great deal of courage, Mr. Collins. You stood up to that well. The pain and feeling of discomfort will fade as the hours pass. You are feeling the worst now. In twelve hours time you will know perfect health and well-being. I promise you that."

"Thank you," Barnabas managed through tight, pain-ridden lips.

Dr. Moreno saw them to the door of the cabin. "It is not every evening that I gain so lucrative a patient. I'm happy to be able to help you, Mr. Collins. After all, that is in keeping with the Hippocratic oath which all we doctors take."

Rita knew his words were a mockery, since she knew the trouble he'd had about his license to practice. Yet, it did seem that he might be able to help Barnabas regardless of his ridiculously high fees. She supposed she should feel grateful.

"Thank you," she told the doctor.

"Glad to be of help," he said as they went out onto the deck where the sounds of revelry from the other cabin came clearly again. "I'll be in touch with you later regarding the changes in the script. I'm sure we can make Brad listen to reason."

She said nothing to this but left the boat with Barnabas. He walked a trifle unsteadily, as if the injection had clouded his brain as well. She began to worry that the unpleasant doctor might have given him something to harm him.

"Are you all right?" she worried as they started up the path to the lawn of Collinwood.

He was staring straight ahead. "A bit dizzy," he said. "It will pass. Whatever he gave me seems to be burning through my veins."

"I hope he knew what he was doing."

"I think so," Barnabas said in a low voice. "My whole body seems to feel more alive in spite of the pain."

Somehow they managed the steep path to the lawn, and because Barnabas seemed so weak and unsteady, she insisted on accompanying him all the way to the old house.

He seemed uneasy about this. "If Joab sees me this way he'll not understand," he said. "He'll think you did something to me."

"I don't care what he thinks," she said grimly. "I'm not leaving you until you're safely at your door."

She stayed with him to the entrance of the old house. There Barnabas halted to offer a weak smile of parting, and when they kissed, his lips were no longer cold. On the contrary, they were hot, as if he was suffering from a burning fever.

"Let me know if you need me," she said to him. "Send Joab."

"You mustn't worry," he told her. "Be careful going back to Collinwood."

She ran most of the way through the misty blackness until she reached the safety of Collinwood. As she entered the old house Brad Hilton came from the living room to greet her in the hallway. He gave her a strange look. "What's wrong? You look frightened to death!"

Rita tried for a smile. "I came back to the house alone. I ran. The darkness scared me."

"And well it might," Brad said with a frown. "Especially with what has been happening to pretty young girls in this area. We don't want you winding up hysterical with teeth-marks on your throat."

"That's not likely to happen," she said.

"It could if you persist in roaming around alone in the dark," the director warned her. "Who were you with? Barnabas Collins?"

"Yes."

"I thought he was the soul of gallantry," Brad said with a wry smile on his battered face. "He might at least have seen you safely home."

"He wasn't feeling well," she said. "I'm worried about him."

"Oh?" the director raised his eyebrows. "Some sudden attack?"

She shrugged, not wanting to go into it. "He hasn't normal health."

"And I can tell you someone who hasn't a normal mentality," Brad said with a hint of anger. "Now David Billings is driving me crazy with complaints. He says I've cut his romantic scenes down to nothing, which isn't true."

"What gave him that idea?"

"Who knows?" Brad said, disgusted. "Actors! I could do without them. He's having one of his sulking spells and I warn you, he blames you. He thinks you wanted the scenes cut to have more footage with Clifton Kerr. And Kerr isn't satisfied! It doesn't make sense!"

"Does this business ever?" she asked.

"Never," he said with a dismal grin. "You get on upstairs and have some sleep. I want you to look your best in the morning."

Feeling somewhat less tense after her short talk with the director, she made her way up the broad stairway to the second floor and her room. She was filled with excitement about the possibilities of the medicine for Barnabas and at the same time worried about the way the injection had left him. Still, the doctor had warned that it could act this way for the first few hours. She'd somehow have to control her feelings and wait it out.

As she passed down the corridor to her room the door next to hers opened and Blanche came out in a dressing gown. "Miss Glenn, do you want me to help you prepare for the night?"

Rita forced a smile. "No, Blanche. I'll manage alone. Thanks just the same."

She went on into her own room, but before she'd turned on the light she felt that cold presence again in the darkness. As she switched on the chandelier she saw that the room was empty—empty except for the betraying scent of violets. The big bedroom was sickeningly sweet with the perfume.

Closing the door she looked around her and said softly, "Angelique."

There was no response, no sound but the distant lash of the waves and the bleating of the foghorn. Then her eyes hit on something, and she went to the dresser. The portrait of herself which she always carried with her and which had been placed on the dresser had been ruthlessly slashed so that the face and shoulders had been obliterated.

She lifted it in her hand and stared at it with thoughtful eyes. And in a small voice she said aloud, "I understand, Angelique. We are bound to be enemies from now on."

CHAPTER 7

When Blanche discovered the slashed photograph the following morning she was in a state of rage. "I tell you, Miss Glenn, it was that nasty Billings who did it. He came here to your room earlier looking for you and I told him you were out."

"I hardly think he'd go that far," Rita said. She was seated before the dresser mirror combing her blonde hair preparatory to donning her costume for the morning's filming.

"Don't you believe he wouldn't!" Blanche raged. "It's just the kind of mean trick I'd expect from him. And I wouldn't mind telling him so to his face."

"We have enough discord in the company without accusations we can't prove," Rita said, convinced that it was the angry spirit of Angelique who was responsible and not the wavy-haired young actor.

Blanche sighed. "Just as you say, miss. But I'll go on thinking he did it just the same."

Rita gave far less thought to the destruction of the photograph than she would have at any other time. Her entire thoughts were on Barnabas and how the serum had worked. Dr. Moreno had seemed to have no doubts that it would restore the Barnabas she loved to normalcy, and this was what she most devoutly desired. But it would be such a miracle that she found it hard to believe it could come true.

Barnabas had seemed really ill when she left him last night. She had never seen him in such a condition. She worried that the medicine might have acted in a different way with him. A serum so strong as the one he'd taken could surely have dire results if it worked against his body rather than with it. Until she saw Barnabas again she would not know an easy moment. Meanwhile it was time to go down for the morning's shots.

Blanche waited with her gown to help her on with it. "You must hurry, miss, or you'll be late," she warned.

In spite of an early morning mist the sun was shining brightly now and it was the kind of lovely July day that only Maine knew, cool and yet warm enough to be enjoyable. The lawn was a beehive of activity as technicians and cameramen moved equipment into place for the morning's scenes.

Rita knew that she was doing one of the big romantic scenes with Clifton Kerr, and the house was to be used as a background. As she appeared on the steps Brad Hilton left a circle of production people to come and greet her.

"I'm glad you're here, Rita," he said. "We're all ready to begin." He smiled. "You look great."

"I don't feel all that good," she said. "I'm nervous." She was wearing an elaborate yellow dress with a wide skirt of the story period.

Brad took her hand and led her over to where the cameras were set up, saying, "You'll forget all about your nervousness once you get to work."

Rita said nothing. The stand-ins for her and Clifton Kerr moved away and she took her place in front of the section of Collinwood that was to be the background for the love scene. She saw David Billings, in costume, standing on the sidelines and gazing at her haughtily. There was no doubt that he was in a mood, she decided with regret. She'd have to speak with him and try and straighten things out.

Clifton Kerr marched onto the set and Dr. Moreno had come to stand with Brad Hilton and watch the scene. Clifton looked dashing in his elaborate costume of another century.

He smiled at her and said, "Why didn't you come to my party last night?"

"I wasn't invited," she said as an excuse.

"I distinctly remember inviting you," he said. "And you were on board, so you knew about it. Moreno told me so."

"Then he should also have told you that I'd taken a patient to see him. And I went home with him."

Clifton Kerr offered her a knowing arrogant smile. "That

Barnabas Collins," he said. "He's not your type."

"He happens to be a good friend," she said coldly. "Don't get all angry about it,"

Clifton cajoled her and he gave her one of his famous smiles, the sort supposed to guarantee any woman's heart. "I'm jealous. I want you to think a bit more about me."

She stared at her co-star. "You have to be joking!"

"I'm serious," he insisted.

The conversation was ended, much to Rita's relief, by Brad calling for the beginning of the scene. It was a delicate romantic interlude early in the picture before she made the discovery that her husband was a slave-trader.

In this sequence all was idyllic love. She knew her lines and Clifton Kerr appeared to know his part well.

For a change, Kerr played the scene without his usual touch of exaggeration. But it was not an easy sequence to capture. Once some trouble with one of the cameras made them repeat a portion that had gone perfectly. When it was repeated it went less well, but Brad doggedly put them through their paces with his untiring enthusiasm.

At last, when they had made the scene four times, he decided it would do and had the cameras move to a new setup on the lawn overlooking the sea. This sequence involved Clifton and David Billings so she was free to take a canvas chair under a sun umbrella and watch the filming.

As she sat there thinking of Barnabas and wondering how he was, a figure came to stand close by her. It was Dr. Moreno. He gazed down at her from behind the sunglasses.

"Your thoughts are far away," he suggested.

She looked up into his demonic face and said, "Perhaps so. I've been wondering how your serum worked on my friend."

"You need not even think of it," the doctor quickly assured her. "He is going to be perfect."

"He seemed very unwell last night," she reminded him.

"I think I made it clear that that was to be expected," the doctor said. "You brought your friend to the right man. Just so long as he can pay my fee."

"The amount you asked seemed extravagantly high," she said.

The doctor shrugged. "Who knows what the price tag should be for a life? I felt I was modest in my request."

"Fortunately it appears that Barnabas Collins is wealthy," Rita said. "So the money makes little difference."

"Had he been a poor man I would have taken that into consideration," the doctor promised.

"I hope you would have," Rita said, though she was certain this wasn't so. In the beginning he'd thought she might pay the two hundred dollars an injection he was demanding.

"What is more important is the way Brad is filming this picture," the doctor said, changing the subject. "I have some definite ideas about a new treatment and I'd like to have you visit the boat and discuss it with Clifton and me."

"I'm satisfied enough as things are," she said.

"But we have an understanding," the doctor reminded her. "In return for my assisting your friend you agreed to take a stand with us."

"He's paying you well enough," she argued.

"This other matter is more important than money," the doctor said firmly. "And I insist that you keep to your part of the bargain."

Rita knew she was trapped, but she said, "We'll let it rest until I find out how Barnabas is."

The doctor laughed softly. "That should not take long," he said. "If I'm not mistaken isn't that him standing on the edge of the set at this very moment."

Rita was sure he was making some kind of unfortunate joke but she strained to look in the direction he'd mentioned and there stood Barnabas smiling at her. She raised a hand to wave to him and he waved back. Better than that, there was a smile on his face.

She glanced up at the doctor. "I don't believe it," she said.

"What did I tell you?" he asked triumphantly.

She got up and hurried over to Brad to ask if she'd be needed for a while. "Barnabas has come to visit the set for the first time," she explained, trying to hide her excitement. "Can I have a quarter-hour free?"

"I suppose so," Brad said grudgingly. And he glanced over where Barnabas was standing. "I hope he doesn't make a habit of this. I don't want anything or anyone interfering with our schedule."

"He won't!" she promised. "This is something special." Without waiting for more words she left the group to join Barnabas.

The tall, dark-haired man had a glow of new health in his face, and as she came up to him he held out his hands to grasp hers. When he took her hand in his she at once felt that they were warm and normal feeling. All the old cold clamminess had vanished.

She stared up at him delightedly. "Barnabas, you look marvelous."

"And I feel marvelous," he said in a happy voice. "It's like being born again."

"I was so frightened last night. You seemed very ill."

"I was," he admitted, a sober light in his eyes. "I wouldn't like to experience hours of pain like that again, but considering my condition this morning, it was worth it."

"It is a miracle," she said. "You have been cured."

He nodded with a wry smile. "At least until my next injection. I shall live in forty-eight hour periods from now on."

"Surely the doctor can do better than that for you," she objected. "He's asking enough for his services."

Barnabas looked troubled. "I don't think it would be wise to argue at this point. We've gained so much more than we hoped for." He glanced towards the set where David Billings and Clifton Kerr were doing their scene again. "Do you have time for a stroll?"

"A short one," she said.

Hand in hand they walked away from the crowd to the quiet of a deserted area of the estate to the rear of the barns. As they walked Barnabas said, "Do you know how many years it has been since I walked under the warm sun?"

She sighed. "Too many."

"And what it's like to really live again?" He tightened his hand on hers and their eyes met in a moment of mutual happiness.

"Of course it means I must immediately have a lot more cash than I've been keeping here in Collinsport," he said. "At two hundred dollars an injection money will vanish quickly."

"Let me help, she said.

"No," he said with a slight frown. "I've worked it all out. After I've had my next injection I'm making a short visit to Boston. I have most of my funds in trust there and I will arrange for a certain amount to be deposited weekly in the Collinsport bank for the time being."

"Have you enough money to keep on with the injections?" she worried.

He halted in the field within sight of the old house and the cemetery down the hill beyond. "I have enough to pay Moreno for a hundred years, and as a normal human being I have no fear of living that long." He smiled at her.

Rita looked up at him, fearful, though smiling. "I'm so happy," she said. "And yet, I'm frightened. Frightened that our happiness should depend on a man like Moreno."

"He'll keep his part of the bargain as long as I pay him," Barnabas said.

"I don't trust him," she said. "He's a cruel, twisted person. Look at the power he has demanded over Kerr in payment for restoring his health."

"I'm not Clifton Kerr," Barnabas told her. "He'll not find it as easy to dominate me. And I have promised to pay him what he has asked."

"Be careful not to let him know too much about your money," she cautioned him. "If he learns how wealthy you really are he'll keep raising his price."

Barnabas nodded towards the cemetery with its rows of ancient tombstones. "I would still consider the gift of life a bargain. Do you realize that all my contemporaries are buried down there? That of them all, I'm the only one alive to see this day."

"Don't!" she protested.

He touched his hand to her arm and smiled in his gentle manner. "You mustn't let my words frighten you. I'm only pointing out how fortunate I feel I am. And how lucky I was to meet you. For without you the miracle wouldn't have happened. You introduced me to the doctor."

"I only hope we don't regret it," she said.

"How can we?" Barnabas demanded. "I'm alive again."

She gave him a strange look. "There's something I've been wanting to ask you," she said. "Did Angelique wear a perfume of wild violets?"

His face shadowed. "Must you ask me about her today of all days?"

"I'm sorry," she said. "Something happened last night that makes me want to know. When I wore a scent of wild violets the other night you said it reminded you of someone."

"It was Josette," he said quietly. "Josette who used that perfume."

"Oh!" she was stunned by the news. She had been so certain it had been the vixen Angelique and instead it was the spirit of the lovely Josette whom Barnabas had adored who'd tormented her. But in consideration this was easily understood. Josette still clung to her love for Barnabas and wanted desperately to keep him among the dead.

"Why have you asked?"

She hesitated, but then told him, ending with the account of the torn photograph. "I'm sorry to bring this up on such a day," she said.

"No," he said, looking concerned. "I'm glad you have told me. And don't hesitate to let me know anything else of this nature that happens. I feel sure it was Josette. And I do not think you should stay in that room alone."

"Surely it's not that serious," she protested.

"It could well be," he cautioned her. "Why don't you arrange for your maid to have a cot in your room and sleep with you for a little while at least."

"She would think it funny," Rita said.

"Tell her your nerves are bad. The strain of the filming," Barnabas suggested. His brow furrowed. "I'll be troubled otherwise. I think Josette is battling you for me, and she will not take this defeat easily."

Rita nodded. "I'll ask Blanche to come to my room if you like."

"It would be best," he assured her. "There are so many things you cannot understand."

"When Dr. Moreno leaves here you'll have to return to Hollywood with him," Rita pointed out. "I have my home in Beverly Hills but you'll have to change your way of living."

"Perhaps we can talk him into giving me quantities of the serum later," Barnabas suggested, "and allowing me to administer my own injections."

"Perhaps," she said. "But he is a strange man. As much as money, he likes power over people."

"I'll be able to deal with him," Barnabas promised. "And now I must take you back." But before he did he took her in his arms for a long kiss, a kiss different from any that had passed between them before, for as his lips caressed hers they were warm and vibrant.

Barnabas took her back to the set and left her after promising to see her at seven that evening. She returned to sit on the sidelines, but it was time to stop for lunch and Brad called a halt to activities until after everyone had taken their noon meal.

He came over to her with a frown on his battered face. "I'd like to have a private talk with you, Rita," he said.

She was surprised. "Of course," she got up.

"Suppose we have lunch served in your room," he suggested. "We can talk up there without being disturbed."

"Anything you like," she said, further mystified.

He left orders for their lunch to be sent upstairs and then joined her in mounting the broad stairway. Not until they were in her room with the door closed after them did he begin to talk to her.

"What is this nonsense about you wanting script changes?" the director asked her.

She had taken the chair by the window overlooking the ocean. "It's not important to me either way," she said weakly, remembering her promise to Dr. Moreno and aware that he might refuse to let Barnabas have the life-giving serum if she didn't insist on the script changes.

Brad shook his head. "I don't understand it. Moreno says you talked to him about the changes, and they're all of a sort to hurt your role in the picture."

"I didn't see it that way," she said.

"Then you're less intelligent than I thought," Brad said bluntly. "I don't want to make the changes, because I feel I have lined the story up in the best possible way. But if all three of you take a stand against me the studio will give in to your demands and the picture will be spoiled."

Rita looked unhappy. "I don't want to cause trouble, Brad. And I surely don't want to hurt my part or ruin the film."

"Then why are you playing Moreno's game?" Brad demanded in despair.

Fortunately she did not have to immediately answer him, for at that moment the waiter arrived with their luncheon and a folding table. It took him a few minutes to set it up and arrange the dishes for them. Not until he had gone and they faced each other across the table did their talk resume.

"A strange mood has come over this company," Brad complained. "We suddenly are faced with all sorts of conflicts."

"I only want to do what is best for everyone," she said.

"David Billings is convinced you've robbed him of scenes," Brad worried. "And my telling him that it isn't so doesn't seem to do any good. There is a sort of madness that's taken hold of everybody."

She forced a smile. "I think you're exaggerating it, Brad."

"You will admit you've talked about script changes to Moreno?" the director said.

Rita hesitated with her salad fork in hand. There was no use in denying this. "Yes," she said. "We did discuss it."

"And you agreed with him, as he says?"

She sighed. "Yes, I'm afraid I did, Brad. But only for the sake of peace. Clifton Kerr is difficult enough to work with at any time. If he's at cross purposes with you he can be impossible. That's what I was thinking of."

The director said, "That's my department. Leave that to me."

"I'm sorry if I made an error," she said.

"It can be corrected," Brad told her, taking a sip of his coffee. "You can simply tell Moreno in front of me that you've decided the script changes would be a mistake."

Fear came into her eyes. She stared at the director. "No,

Brad. I can't do that!"

The director gazed at her incredulously. "Rita, what kind of talk is that?"

She knew they had reached an impasse. Wearily she said, "Please, Brad, I don't want to talk about it now."

"I see," he said and lapsed into a gloomy silence that lasted through the balance of the meal.

That afternoon it remained bright and work on the film continued. Rita was involved only a part of the time and while she sat on the sidelines she did a good deal of thinking. It would take a week or two to find out how Barnabas fared on the new treatments. She could only hope the cure would be permanent and the sinister Moreno would continue to cooperate in giving them on the terms he'd agreed upon but she couldn't be sure.

Once she knew which way things were going she could take a stronger stand on her own. She felt guilty about having let Brad Hilton down and as soon as she felt Barnabas was safe she meant to let Moreno know that she wouldn't be bullied by him. But that had to wait.

She watched Moreno as he sat studying Brad's every move in directing the scenes and noticed the frequent whispered exchanges between the wily doctor and Clifton Kerr. The two of them were up to no good. And she was also surprised to see that Kerr was paying a great deal of attention to one of the pretty brunette script girls. She learned from a worker on the set that this was the girl who'd been mysteriously attacked.

It made her nervous to see Kerr and the girl so friendly. And she worried that Moreno might have told Kerr about Barnabas and now the actor was trying to discover if the girl had any memory of who'd placed the teeth-marks on her throat. She wouldn't put it past the actor to cue the girl as to who had been responsible and cause trouble for Barnabas.

But surely Dr. Moreno wouldn't allow him to do that since he was in a position to gain so much financially by treating Barnabas. It all left her very much on edge and she was glad she was not taking a big part in the day's filming.

Finally the day came to an end and she breathed a sigh of relief. At seven that evening Barnabas arrived promptly to meet her. She borrowed a station wagon from the crew and they drove into Collinsport and stopped by the noisy Blue Whale for a while. Brad Hilton was there and he came up to the booth where they were seated and greeted them with a wry smile.

"It's not often we see you two out on the town," he observed. "You keep mostly to yourselves."

Rita returned his smile. "Barnabas is feeling much better

and we're celebrating."

"Good," Brad said. And he gave his attention to Barnabas. "While your girlfriend is in such a mellow mood I wish you'd give her a little advice. Tell her to stay away from that Moreno."

Barnabas was surprised. "What do you mean?"

"She can explain," Brad said cryptically and with a nod left them to go back to the bar.

Barnabas gave her a questioning look. "I don't understand why he should mention Dr. Moreno. Does he know about me?"

"Of course not," Rita said. "It's something else."

But Barnabas was not to be put off. "He must think it has something to do with me or he wouldn't have deliberately brought it up that way when we were together."

She hesitated. "It's nothing. Moreno asked me to take sides with him and Clifton Kerr in some changes he wants in the script."

"He wants you to take sides against Brad?"

"Yes."

"And you're doing it?"

She shrugged. "I don't feel it is all that important," she said, trying to sound casual.

Barnabas studied her with his penetrating eyes. "Brad seems to think it is important," he said gravely.

"For goodness sake," she expostulated, "let's forget it. It's movie business and has nothing to do with us. We're out for an evening's fun."

"I believe there's more to it than you're admitting," he said. "I suspect it's some deal Moreno made you agree to before he would treat me."

"Barnabas!" she said, giving him a pleading look.

"I don't want you making any such bargains," he told her sharply, and added impatiently, "Let's get out of here."

They left the crowded Blue Whale for a drive along the shore. There was a moon and when they came to a turnout with an excellent view of the ocean they parked and enjoyed the beauty of the night.

Barnabas had his arm around her. "I'm very worried about what Brad said," he told her.

"Please don't let it spoil things," she begged. "I don't want to risk your cure in any way."

"I still intend to have a straight talk with Moreno," Barnabas said evenly.

She pressed her head against his shoulder, aware of the warmth of his body as she gazed out at the silver ocean under the giant moon. "How lucky we are!" she said.

"And think what the future can hold for us."

"I'm not happy in the old house any longer," he confessed. "Its grime and age repel me now. If I continue to remain normal I will have to find a new place to live."

"At least you need no longer go near that awful room with the coffin," she said.

He smiled. "Now. Now my sleeping hours are at night. As normal as those of anyone else. Joab is still thunderstruck. He does not understand what has happened."

"Will you keep him on?"

"I feel I should," Barnabas said. "The poor fellow has been very faithful to me."

"But he is so strange," she said.

"He cannot help his affliction," Barnabas told her. "And I'm sure he will become less suspicious and aggressive now that he is no longer responsible for me."

"Perhaps that is true," she agreed, snuggling closer to him. "And you're such a different person now, Barnabas."

"I enjoy a great deal more freedom," he said. "After I have my second injection I shall make my brief visit to Boston."

She raised her head to stare at him with concern. "Do you think you dare, so soon?"

"The second injection will take care of me for two full days," he reminded her. "And I do need to free some funds to pay Moreno."

"It's ridiculous what he's asking."

Barnabas smiled sadly. "Since he has the power to give or withdraw life I cannot haggle."

"And please don't get into any argument with him on my account," she begged.

Barnabas drew her close to him again. "I will use discretion, be sure of that. I do not want to lose you and that is what withdrawal of the serum would mean."

They kissed and then drove back to Collinwood. The time had gone quickly and it was close to midnight. After the car was parked Barnabas saw her to the door. They said goodnight and he spoke of going into the village in the morning to do some shopping. He had an enormous appetite and he was encouraging Joab to improve his cooking, so extra provisions were needed.

Rita went inside and found the house deathly silent.

Only the night light was on for the stairs. She was about to go up to her room when she heard a distant scream, the high-pitched cry of a frightened woman. She hesitated on the stairs, a shadow crossing her face.

At another time she might have worried that it was

Barnabas assaulting some poor creature in his thirst for blood, but she knew he no longer had that need now. So what did the cry mean? Filled with a troubled curiosity she went back down the stairs and outside to the steps. She'd only been standing there a minute when she saw a figure looming out of the darkness. And he was coming towards her.

CHAPTER 8

For no reason she could clearly understand the sight of the man approaching her froze her with fear. She stood there staring into the darkness and unable to move. It took her a long moment to identify who it was and then she recognized Clifton Kerr.

Kerr came up to the steps and offered her a mocking smile. "I didn't expect to find anyone as pretty as you here," he said.

Some of her fear vanished although she still felt uneasy. "I heard a scream. It sounded like a girl. I came out to try and find out what it might mean."

Kerr looked amused. "Your nerves are bad. You've been listening to the cry of a night bird and are imagining things."

She gave him a troubled look. "Do you really think so?"

"I've been strolling in the moonlight and that's all I've heard," he told her.

"It must have been my imagination," she said and turned to go inside.

Kerr reached out and grasped her arm. "Don't leave me so soon. I've been wanting someone to talk to. My nerves are wound up after the day's filming and I wasn't able to sleep."

Rita resented his abrupt grabbing of her arm, but she realized he was in a kind of high, excited mood and probably wasn't able to sleep. Against her better judgment she allowed him to lead her down to the lawn.

"Let's walk as far as the cliff and back. It's a spot that fascinates me," he suggested.

Since it was only a short distance and well within sight of the house she didn't feel she could refuse, though she would have much preferred to have gone inside and up to bed. She had followed the advice Barnabas had given her and asked Blanche to sleep on a cot in her room, and she knew Blanche would be worried about her being out so late.

She said, "I can't stay out long. We have an early call in the morning. Remember?"

Clifton Kerr gave her a thin smile as they strolled across the lawn toward the path leading to the cliff. He said, "I don't know whether I'll bother to report for work tomorrow morning or not. I may sleep late."

Rita frowned. "You wouldn't hold up production that way!"

"Let Brad shoot around my scenes," Kerr said indifferently. "He's lucky I decided to do this picture."

"I think since you've agreed to do it you should give him your best," she said.

"I'm an artist not a workhorse," Clifton Kerr said airily. "I'll let Moreno settle it with him."

She said, "It seems to me you allow Moreno to decide too much for you."

He gave her a sharp glance. "I owe everything to Moreno. Without him I wouldn't be a star today."

"But isn't he using you now?" she insisted. "Taking more than his share of your earnings?"

Clifton Kerr's famous profile showed a wicked grin in the moonlight. "If you think he's such an unscrupulous person why do you refer your friends to him?"

Rita's cheeks flamed. "I can consider him wily and still have respect for his talents."

"I advise you to have respect for him in every way if you look for him to continue treating your friend, Barnabas Collins," the actor said sarcastically.

They were soon strolling along the path that ran close to the cliff's edge and the pounding of the waves could be heard below. Rita halted and stared at him with concern. "What did Dr. Moreno tell you about Barnabas?"

Clifton Kerr's eyebrows raised. "Nothing, except that he'd taken him on as a patient. I never question Dr. Moreno about his personal affairs."

Rita felt a small relief. She believed the actor because she wanted to. She could not face that the sinister doctor would leak the news about the terrible demon that possessed Barnabas.

She said, "I guess I shouldn't have brought his name up."

"You'll learn," Kerr predicted.

"I know he has great talent," she said. "Don't think I'm blind to that. It's just that I dislike him as a person."

"Many people say the same thing about me," Kerr said carelessly. "And probably about you if you only knew it."

She smiled bitterly as they continued to stroll towards the jutting point of the cliff. "It is fortunate we don't hear others' opinions of ourselves. Of course, in our profession we can't escape the candor of the critics."

"I never read them anymore," Clifton Kerr said. "They have nothing to offer me."

"I don't feel that way about all of them," Rita argued. "Some of them have very good ideas."

He gave her another of his cynical smiles as they reached the point and came to a halt. "I'm beginning to think you're a romantic, ill-equipped to deal with this rather cold world."

"It could be," she admitted, admiring the view of the cove by moonlight and the distant beam of Collinsport lighthouse.

"Barnabas Collins will never make a suitable husband for you," Clifton Kerr said. "You should marry in the profession. Preferably someone like me."

She gave a small laugh. "Surely you must be joking!"

The good-looking actor appeared annoyed. "Is the idea of me as a husband so amusing to you?"

"But we're such different types," she said. "And you have so much ego and temperament. I doubt if you'd make a likely marriage partner for anyone."

Kerr was still in his high mood. "I'm not unduly cast down by your unflattering opinion of me," he said. "There are lots of other girls ready to line up to be Mrs. Clifton Kerr."

"I don't doubt it."

"Why not you?"

She smiled wanly. "Perhaps you don't have the same glamor for me. I've worked in the film world long enough to know it for what it is."

"An interesting observation," he said. "But then what possible attraction can a person like Barnabas Collins have for you?"

"I'm very fond of Barnabas," she warned him. "So please don't speak against him."

Kerr shrugged. "Everyone to their taste. I'd find him reserved and too much old world for me. I'll admit he's not bad-looking."

"He's handsome," she said defiantly.

His eyes met hers. "In a gaunt, unusual way," he said, and he said it in a way that again made her wonder if Moreno had told him Barnabas was suffering from the vampire curse.

"I find his looks pleasing," she said.

"You haven't given yourself a chance to know me," Clifton Kerr taunted her. "You'd find I have a lot more charm. And I don't live in some crummy, cobwebby house with a crazy servant."

"Barnabas has his work. The house suits him."

"What sort of work?" Clifton Kerr asked her jeeringly.

She felt new panic, certain now that Kerr knew more than he was admitting. She said, "In any case he plans to move soon."

"I'd think that would be wise. I couldn't bear those surroundings myself."

She said, "It's time I went back."

"Come on," he insisted. "You're not a little girl reporting to her governess. You're a grown-up movie star." He grasped her by the arm again.

"Please let me go," she begged him.

He continued to grip her. "And if I don't, what do you propose to do, scream?" he taunted her. "That won't do you any good up here."

"Stop joking!" she said, fear in her eyes. "You're hurting my arm."

But he made no move to release her; if anything, his fingers became more steel-like. Now he bent close with intensity, his eyes wildly bright. "I'm in love with you and you treat me as if I were some bit player in the company."

"You're drunk!" she protested. "Let me go!"

"If I'm drunk it's because of passion for you," he said thickly. "Rita, we could make the starring team of the century. We could share the world together. Carve it up between us!"

"I don't want to hear any more," she cried, struggling to free herself.

But there was no escape, and he brought her close and embraced her, his lips pressing hard against hers in spite of her attempts to avoid them. And she was conscious of his cold lips and heavy, offensive breath.

Finally he released her with a mocking laugh. "You'll learn to love me," he promised. "Give yourself time!"

"You're insane!" she sobbed and she turned to race back along the path towards Collinwood.

For a moment she thought he was following her, but he wasn't. Still she continued to run for the safety of the house. The experience she'd just had with the arrogant leading man had been almost unbelievable. The feel of his cold lips was still on hers and she brushed a hand across to wipe away the last trace of his repugnant kiss. His fetid, disgusting breath had also repelled her.

She could not imagine him taking the liberties he had unless he knew about Barnabas and was using this knowledge to blackmail her into accepting his advances. He and the odious Dr. Moreno were so close that she doubted there were any secrets not shared between them. Kerr must know about Barnabas. That was why he'd been so brash as to behave as he had just now. He counted on her silence to protect the man she loved.

She did not dare tell Barnabas, just as she hadn't fully informed him about Dr. Moreno's blackmailing activities. He'd guessed some of it, thanks to Brad's tip-off in the tavern, but she wouldn't let him know more. He might even refuse to go on using the serum. There was, however, no longer any doubt in her mind that her attempt to save Barnabas had landed them in the power of two completely amoral persons.

Blanche was asleep when Rita entered her bedroom and she quietly prepared for bed so as not to disturb her. Barnabas had been worried about the menace of Josette's spirit, but the biggest threat appeared to be coming from the wily doctor and the arrogant leading man. She lay awake a long while thinking about all that had taken place and wondering how she could cope with a situation which was growing increasingly difficult for her.

True to his prediction, Clifton Kerr did not appear on the set the following morning. Dr. Moreno came and had a brief discussion with Brad Hilton and then left without even saying hello to her. Rita could tell that Brad was upset about the leading man not showing up since all the planned scenes for that day had included him.

He came across to where she was sitting with Blanche, a disgusted look on his face. "That just about does it," he complained. "Kerr is reporting ill and I don't know when he'll be back."

She said, "We'll have to do the scenes he's not in."

"That would be easy," the director said. "Except we're not prepared for them. I have to line up a complete new schedule and get properties and lights in place. Everyone will have the morning off. I'll try to do the scenes with you and David Billings this afternoon."

It was the beginning of a difficult day. By the time Brad did get an interior scene in the living room properly lit and the cameras in place a good part of the afternoon had passed. In addition, David Billings was still sulking and gave a miserable lackadaisical performance which enraged Brad. When the director complained and made them repeat the scene the blond young man blew up in his lines and had a mild case of hysterics. That ended work for the day.

Rita felt exhausted, but she was eager to talk with Barnabas again. It had been decided between them that he would go to the boat and get his injection from Moreno on his own. Then he would meet her at Collinwood a little after nine. If he felt unwell again he could go directly back to the old house and endure the effects of the serum.

Knowing how much he had suffered from the initial injection Rita worried that the second one might be equally incapacitating. In fact, she told Barnabas not to try to meet her at all if he really felt ill. She was more concerned with his health than their having the evening together.

But he did arrive shortly after nine. She had been waiting for him and as they left Collinwood, she asked, "How are you?"

"It was exactly as he promised," Barnabas said. "I haven't even felt the second injection."

"Then you're going to be all right," she said, pleased at this news.

He glanced down at her. "Providing Moreno doesn't change his mind about giving me the injections. He appeared in a sullen mood tonight."

She showed a tiny frown. "I hope you didn't bother him about that script business."

"I did mention it and he denied it," Barnabas said. "He claims he had put no pressure on you at all. Is that true?"

Rita knew she couldn't tell him the truth. She evaded a direct reply by saying, "I warned you that you misunderstood the situation."

"I still want to have you keep me informed," Barnabas told her.

"I will. I promise," she said. They had been walking out across the lawn without any general direction in mind and soon found themselves near the edge of the cliff.

He halted, facing her in the darkness. "I plan to leave for Boston early in the morning," he said. "I may not be able to return until just before time for my next dose of serum the following evening."

The thought of him leaving Collinwood alarmed her. "I'll be worried every moment you're away," she told him.

He smiled. "No need for you to be. I'll be completely all right. And I must look after that money business."

"I'm thinking of myself as much as of you," she admitted. "I don't like being left alone here."

"Hardly alone," he said. "You're surrounded by the entire

company."

"I'll still feel alone without you," she said. "Brad was right. There is something brooding about the atmosphere here." And then she gave him a searching look and asked, "Barnabas, could there possibly be any other vampires in this area?"

Barnabas stared at her. "Why do you ask that?"

"After you left me last night I heard what I'm sure was a female cry for help." She paused. "I couldn't help thinking how things used to be and that someone might be facing attack." Glancing up at him she went on earnestly, "I know it couldn't be you now. So I wondered."

"It must have been some other sort of cry you heard," he said. "I know of no one here aside from me who suffered the same sort of curse."

She sighed. "It could have been my imagination. I've been terribly nervous lately."

"And no wonder," he said with gentleness. "But you need not fear any longer. Each day I improve. And when I return I'll have plenty of cash to pay Moreno."

"That scoundrel!" she said angrily.

"It could be that one day we'll find another answer to my condition and so be free of him," Barnabas told her. "In the meantime we have to play it his way."

Their evening together was brief. Barnabas saw her back to Collinwood and kissed her goodnight on the steps and waited to see her safely inside. The night was uneventful and the following day Clifton Kerr did not show up for work again. This was especially annoying to everyone since the weather was good and there was no telling how long it might last.

Brad had to be content to go over the scenes in the living room between Rita and Billings. With a fresh morning start they went better. And as they finished just before lunch Rita was surprised to discover that Dr. Moreno had been seated beside Brad during most of the takes and watching them with great interest.

The doctor came over to her. "A fine performance, Rita," he said. "I thoroughly enjoyed it."

"How long before Clifton makes up his mind to work again?" she asked.

"That is up to him," he said coolly. "He is not well."

"He's probably drinking too much," she scoffed.

"You are not being charitable," Moreno observed sadly.

"I don't think of charity where Clifton Kerr is concerned," she said. "He has little for anyone else."

Dr. Moreno smiled. "You have an acid tongue, Rita. You should take care it doesn't land you in trouble."

"I try to be truthful," she said.

"Even truth can be a vice," he warned her. "I'd like to have a talk with you on board this evening. And don't tell me you can't come. I happen to know that Barnabas is out of town."

"I'd rather not come," she said.

"But you will," he said. "I think we should make it about eight."

And before she could offer any other arguments he'd left. Knowledge of the evening meeting worried her. It was not by accident the sinister doctor had chosen the evening Barnabas was away to request her to visit him. She was standing there watching after him when someone came up beside her. It was C. Stanton Shaw, still in costume.

Presenting a suitable appearance for the ancient house in his elegant old-fashioned clothes, he smiled grimly to Rita. "You are not picking your company too carefully these days, Miss Glenn."

She turned to him with a frown. "I don't follow you."

"I had no idea you and our doctor friend were on such good terms," the old actor said in his harsh voice.

"We're not."

"Oh?" He raised his eyebrows. "I've noticed him talking to you a good deal lately."

"I've tried to discourage him," she said. "He's a rather persistent person."

"And he's to blame for Clifton Kerr not reporting for work," the old man snorted. "It's his method of forcing Brad to change the script. You wait and see. As soon as Brad agrees to the changes he's been demanding, Kerr will come back to work again."

"I can't believe they'd plot that openly," Rita said.

"Then you don't know Moreno," Shaw said. "And watch that he doesn't involve you in it. That's what he's likely up to."

"I'll be careful," she promised.

The old actor nodded his head. "I'd like to see this picture completed and become a success, but I don't think Moreno or Kerr care."

She thought about this later when she was alone, and decided that she would not meekly assent to anything the sinister Dr. Moreno suggested when she visited him that evening. She had her own career to protect and she owed Brad loyalty. The business with Barnabas should be kept apart from the filming. Barnabas was paying the doctor well for his services.

She was lonesome without Barnabas and wondered how he was making out in the city. The time between dinner and her meeting with Moreno weighed heavily on her. And since it was a pleasant evening she decided to take a walk before going down to the boat. Without thinking, she made her way toward the old house as if her longing for Barnabas had decided it.

As she drew near the bleak stone house she could not help thinking how desolate it appeared. No wonder Barnabas was impatient to leave it now that he had become a normal human being again. The remembrance of that dark room in the cellar with its casket made her shudder. At least Barnabas was saved from that, no matter what else they endured from the hateful Dr. Moreno.

She had almost reached the house when a figure emerged from the front entrance and came down the steps. Rita recognized Joab. His head was bent, the short, gray hairs flaring out wildly from the broad skull. Because he was proceeding along the path in her direction, it was inevitable that they should meet.

Bracing herself, she made up her mind to show no fear. Then Joab was close to her so that she could see his malevolent red-streaked eyes fixed on her. As they passed he made a low growling sound as if a sudden move on her part would be all that was required to have him attack her. She hid her fear and continued on.

Drawing a breath of relief that the meeting was over, she continued on down the hill to the cemetery as if some unseen force was directing her steps there. She worried about Joab's hatred and wondered how she could make him lose his distrust of her. Barnabas was fond of him and wanted to keep him in his employ, but Rita wondered if she could ever become used to him. More importantly, would he ever accept her?

As her thoughts came back to the moment at hand, she realized she was already inside the cemetery with its iron fence and pointed ornamental spikes at intervals. She weaved her way between the tombstones in the fading light, recalling her last meeting there with Barnabas. It had been then that she'd persuaded him to visit Dr. Moreno. She hoped that she had done right.

The weathered tombstones on all sides of her bore birthdates and the death days of all the people at Collinwood who had been alive when the curse had first been placed on Barnabas. Because of the curse, he alone walked the earth now. And if he continued to take the serum he would eventually die a normal death as she would in time. It was what he wanted. A release from the long nightmare of wandering the darkness of centuries searching for soft throats and warm blood.

She found herself standing before the weathered gray stone with the name Josette almost obliterated from it. Josette who had loved Barnabas long ago and was reluctant to let him pass back into a living state now. She stared at the worn lettering and as she did so the air was all at once filled with the scent of wild violets!

Josette's perfume! The thought struck terror in her as

she realized how defenseless and isolated she was in that lonely cemetery. A chill had gathered around her and for a moment she could not move. Then she turned and ran screaming for the cemetery gate. In her terror and haste she missed the way and instead came upon the iron fence. She stumbled and fell, coming within inches of impaling her slim young body on one of the ornamental spikes.

She lay there breathing heavily, fearful as she eyed the fence and realized the narrowness of her escape. Suddenly, from the tall evergreens behind the cemetery, there suddenly darted a black bat-like creature which flew down close to her and she covered her face for protection and cried out again. It hovered above her a moment and then vanished in the dark forest from which it came.

Sobbing with fear, Rita rose weakly and found her way to the cemetery gate and freedom from the menacing unknown that had threatened her there. She touched a handkerchief to her eyes as she started back up the hill and, taking her compact from her pocket, did her best to repair her make-up. It had been stupid of her to venture near the cemetery alone after the warning Barnabas had given her. She could not help glancing over her shoulder from time to time as she hurried back toward Collinwood, wary that some phantom creature might be following her.

It was close to eight o'clock, so she went directly down the path to the wharf and the boat. Dr. Moreno was waiting for her alone in his cabin and welcomed her in his usual urbane manner.

When she had seated herself, she said, "I'm anxious to get back to the house. Will you please quickly tell me what you want."

The man with the dark glasses and swarthy skin sat facing her. He smiled. "I'm not sure that I can explain things to you in a hurry."

"Why have you asked me here?"

"To make sure you understand certain matters," he said evenly.

"Such as?"

"That you do owe me a debt for taking on your friend Barnabas as a patient," the doctor said sharply. "Cases of his type are not easy to treat. You would find no one else willing to take care of him."

"He is paying you an exorbitant fee."

"You may think so. I don't," Moreno said. "I have a statement concerning Brad's handling of the direction of this film which I'm sending to the studio. I'd like your signature on it along with mine and Clifton's before I send it."

"If it's something detrimental to Brad I can't sign it," she said. "He is one of the few persons in this business I respect."

Moreno looked sullen. "Is that your final word?"

"I'm afraid it is."

"You realize this may influence my decision to treat Mr. Collins."

She smiled bitterly. "I doubt it. You won't pass up the money he offers."

The eyes behind the dark glasses regarded her coldly. "You take that very much for granted."

"I think I understand you well enough for that, Dr. Moreno," she said, rising. "If that's all you wanted to see me about, there's no need for me to remain."

"But there is," the swarthy man said, also standing now. "I wish to discuss Clifton Kerr with you."

This was something of a surprise. "Discuss him in what way?"

The doctor shrugged. "It's a most delicate matter, but I think I should point out that he has a rather deep romantic interest in you. Don't ask me why. But it seems to have become an obsession with him."

"That's too bad," she said. "He doesn't interest me."

"Come now, Rita," Moreno said with a nasty smile. "He's not all that unpleasant. Half the women in the country are in love with his screen image."

"It's not a matter of whether he's pleasant or unpleasant," she said. "I'm not in love with him. As you well know, I love Barnabas Collins."

The sinister doctor nodded. "So you do. Then it is Barnabas who stands in the way."

She felt a surge of fear. "It wouldn't make any difference if Barnabas was here or not. I still couldn't bring myself to care for Clifton Kerr!"

"I wonder," the doctor said softly.

"I mean it," she insisted. "I don't know what is behind Kerr's supposed sudden interest in me but I resent it."

"Kerr is my protege," the doctor reminded her. "My creation, if you like, and he is used to my granting him his wishes."

"There are some wishes beyond even your powers," Rita told him bitterly.

The doctor sighed. "I dislike telling him how you feel. I know it won't go well with him. And he'll try to persuade me to break my contract with your friend, Barnabas Collins."

"And forfeit all the money he is willing to pay for the serum," Rita said. "Not likely."

The doctor gave her a wry smile. "There might be other ways of my cashing in on Mr. Collins," he said. "I think I could sell his story for a good sum to the press. It might even pay me more to expose him for what he is than to treat him."

Rita was shocked. She stared at the doctor in alarm. "You wouldn't do a thing like that!"

"You underestimate me," he assured her quietly. "I will do anything to gain my own ends. So I suggest you think over all that I have said to you."

She stood there, knowing she should leave, yet hesitating to go after hearing him deliver such an ultimatum. "I can't believe that even you can be so evil."

"My reputation has been hard won," he said with a cold smile. "I never hesitate to destroy anything that stands in my way. And that's not merely a repeating of a trite phrase. I mean it."

There was little doubt in her mind that he did. She might as well accept it; she had been checkmated by a master. "I'm sorry if I've offended you. I hope you won't take it out on Barnabas," she said, and turned to leave the cabin.

He followed her out onto the deck. "I don't mind your not signing that letter for Hollywood," he said. "But I advise you to think over your relationship with Clifton Kerr. I'm sure that if you take the right attitude you'll find him charming."

She made no answer. There was nothing for her to say. She made her way along the wharf and up the path towards the house. Standing at the edge of the cliff waiting for her was a man in a trenchcoat. As she drew near she saw it was Brad Hilton.

His face wore an ironic smile. "So you've been partaking of Dr. Moreno's hospitality," he said.

"I stopped by to see him for a moment," she said stiffly.

Brad studied her penetratingly. "I hope you know the rules. Moreno asks a high price of those he entertains."

She looked at him in alarm. "Brad, don't get any wrong ideas. I need your friendship."

"You have it," he said, staring at her. "The question is do I have yours?"

They stood there into the darkness and she drew her tweed coat around her against the chill of the night and as a gesture to fend off the cold fear pressing hard on her heart.

"You have my friendship, Brad," she said. "I give you my word."

He nodded down where the power boat with its portholes showing light was tied to the small wharf. "Then what did that mean?"

"He wanted to see me," she said dully. "I had to go."

"He's trying to get you to join him and Kerr in complaining to the studio, isn't that it?" Brad asked.

She sighed and stared down at her feet. "He talked about it. I turned him down."

"Thanks," Brad said dryly. "I'll know that definitely when I hear from Hollywood. What hold does Moreno have on you?"

Rita looked up at him with startled eyes. "What do you mean?"

"You wouldn't be so friendly with him if there wasn't some reason," the director insisted. "Has it anything to do with this Collins fellow?"

"Why do you ask that?"

"Because I saw him visiting the boat last night," Brad informed her. "What is his connection with Moreno?"

She shrugged. "He has consulted him for medical advice."

Brad looked cynical. "Everyone knows Moreno is the worst kind of charlatan."

"He cured Clifton Kerr."

"I sometimes wonder what the cure was worth," the director said. "You see the kind of person he is today. That's what Moreno's influence has done for him."

"Still he is a doctor," Rita argued. "He does know about many strange tropical diseases."

Brad studied her in silence for a moment. Then he asked, "Just what ails your friend Barnabas Collins that he should be forced to consult a quack like Moreno?"

"I don't know," she said despairingly.

Brad gave her a hard look. "I doubt that," he said. "And I wonder if it isn't some mental disturbance. I can't imagine any sane man living in that old house thick with dust, without electricity or proper heat, and with only that weird mute manservant for company."

"Barnabas is a fine, intelligent man," she insisted.

"So you say," Brad told her with a thin smile of doubt. "But I have my own ideas and so have others. Do you know that the attacks on girls around here have resumed?"

"No, I hadn't heard about it," she said in a frightened voice. And at the same time she recalled the cry she had heard the other night.

"A village girl was assaulted not far from Collinwood and found wandering in a semiconscious state with those odd teeth-marks on her throat," Brad said. "The police are beginning to think it is the work of a maniac. Someone living in Collinsport."

"Oh?" she said faintly.

Brad nodded in a grim fashion. "And I'd say either Barnabas Collins or his servant could be considered first-class suspects."

"You shouldn't say that. It couldn't have been Barnabas. Not the other night!"

"Why are you so positive of it?"

She hesitated guiltily, realizing she might have spoken too quickly. "I'm just sure of it, that's all."

"I have an idea the police will want to ask Mr. Barnabas Collins some pertinent questions when he returns from his Boston trip," Brad said. "And if you're hoping Moreno will cover up for him, I wouldn't."

"I don't want to hear anything more about it," she exclaimed and she rushed past him to make her way across the lawn to Collinwood.

She had a miserable night, worrying about what both the doctor and Brad had said. It seemed that one way or another Barnabas was going to be exposed to serious trouble. Just now when he could begin a new life. It didn't seem fair.

Blanche fussed over her appearance as Rita got into her costume the following morning. "I declare, you look like you didn't sleep a wink," her dresser said.

Rita smiled wanly. "You're wrong. I slept most of the night." It wasn't true, but she didn't dare allow Blanche to guess that.

"You're pale and you've lost weight. I don't think Maine has agreed with you," Blanche said as she zipped the dress up the back.

"Don't worry," Rita said. "The picture will soon be finished and we'll be on our way back to Hollywood."

"Not if Clifton Kerr keeps holding up production, we won't," Blanche huffed. "We've lost two good days because of him already."

And they were to lose a third. He didn't turn up for work that morning. And they had barcly started on a substitute outdoor scene when it began to shower. Once again Brad had to issue the order that work was at an end for the day.

Rita was on edge for the evening to arrive and Barnabas to get back. She wanted to tell him what was happening and warn him about what Brad had said. The showers continued throughout the day, so she was confined to the house, and when the showers ended in the evening the fog came again.

It was nine thirty when Barnabas arrived. Most of the others had gone to the village so they had the big living room to themselves. Rita took him to a divan in a remote corner of it and, seating herself beside him, began to question him in a low voice.

"Did your Boston trip turn out well?" she asked.

Barnabas nodded. "Yes. I have the financial arrangements all made and I just received my third injection from Dr. Moreno."

Rita gave him a frightened look. "Barnabas, something ugly is going on here. Clifton Kerr has been behaving strangely, making overtures to me and not reporting for work. And Dr. Moreno has been trying to persuade me to take Kerr's attentions seriously."

Barnabas looked at her incredulously. "Why should he do that?"

"I don't know," she confessed. "And another girl has been attacked. Since you've been given your treatments. Brad says they suspect someone here at Collinwood and hinted it might be you or Joab."

His eyes narrowed. "So there's been an attack since I've been taking the serum."

"Yes," she said. "I almost began to fear the serum hadn't worked. That it was you again."

"No!" He shook his head. "It has to be someone else. You were right when you had suspicions there was another person suffering from the vampire curse in the area. There has to be if the attacks are continuing."

"But who?" she asked.

"I can't imagine," he said, frowning. "Unless someone is deliberately imitating my original attacks to get me in trouble. It could be Moreno. He knows all about the curse and could simulate such an attack."

"He's capable of deliberately doing it," she agreed. "What can we manage to protect you?"

"Nothing, yet," Barnabas decided. "We'll wait and see if the attacks go on."

"But the police may come after you any tune! Or Joab!"

"We'll have to risk that," he said, taking her hands in his and gazing at her solemnly. "Depend on me. I'll find a way out of this. Don't you do a thing."

CHAPTER 9

Rita had no idea then how difficult it would be to follow the advice of the man she loved. But events were soon to place her in a worse predicament than she ever had imagined. It began the following morning. And as if to suggest what was to come, the day began with a thick fog.

She had barely finished her breakfast and was still in her dressing gown when there was a knock on her bedroom door. Blanche opened it and Brad was standing there, grave-faced.

"May I come in for a moment?"

"Of course," she said.

The director glanced towards Blanche and then looked at her again. "I'd like to speak with you privately."

"Very well," she said. She nodded to Blanche and the maid left them. Then she said, "What is it? You look very solemn."

"I'm afraid this time it's murder," Brad said.

Rita jumped up. "Murder?"

"Yes. You remember the script girl. The pretty little brunette who was attacked once before. She was throttled last night just a short distance from Collinwood. And those same weird teeth marks were on her throat!"

"The poor girl!" Rita said in dismay. "I saw her on the set only the other day. She was chatting with Clifton Kerr. She was a beauty."

"She's in the morgue now," Brad said grimly. "And this time the fat is really in the fire. The state police are moving in to make a thorough investigation."

"They should," Rita said. "The killer must be found."

Brad studied her. "I wonder that you're so strong on that," he said. "As I remember it, Barnabas Collins returned from Boston last night."

She caught her breath. "You're not suggesting Barnabas did this awful thing?"

"I'm not suggesting anything," Brad said curtly. "I'm only telling you that Barnabas was at Collinwood last night and he can be considered a suspect. He likely will be!"

"But I'm positive he didn't do it!"

"How can you be?" Brad demanded.

"You'll have to believe me," she implored. "Barnabas is the last person to be guilty of this."

"He'll have a chance to convince the police," Brad said grimly. "They are poking through everything. Even if we had good weather and Clifton Kerr wasn't bucking me we'd not be able to do any filming until this thing is settled. The company is in shock. That girl was a favorite with everyone."

"I'm sorry, Brad," she said sincerely.

He frowned. "I haven't been able to get it all straightened out in my mind," he said, "but I have a hunch you know a lot more than you're telling me. And if you are trying to protect this Barnabas, knowing he's guilty, it could go hard for you."

With that the director left her. She felt ill but she knew she had to get to Barnabas without delay. It was possible he didn't know about the crime yet. And she wanted him to have some warning.

Dressing quickly, she headed for the old stone house. On the way she saw several of the state policemen moving about the grounds. Brad was right. They were making a complete check of everything. When she reached the ancient mansion she used the doorknocker and waited for someone to answer.

Barnabas opened the door himself, and she saw at once that he had heard the news and the police had probably already visited him. He was pale and his expression was grave.

"Come in," he invited her quickly. "Did they see you coming here? The police, I mean."

"I don't know," she said, entering the dark, damp hallway. "I guess so."

He glanced out furtively before closing the door to leave them in the dank hall in almost complete darkness. He spoke in a low urgent voice, "At least they aren't following you. I see no sign of them."

"Have they been here?"

"Yes. They gave me some grilling," Barnabas told her, taking her gently by the elbow and leading her into the dust-covered living room where at least there was some murky light. They stood facing each other tensely.

"Who could have murdered that poor girl?" she asked him.

"I've been doing a lot of thinking about that," he said. "At least for the time being I've convinced them it wasn't me."

"Good," she said.

"But I have a hunch they still consider me the most logical suspect," he said. "And if I don't turn up the real murderer they'll be back. And the next time it won't be so easy to get rid of them."

"I'm so afraid!" she said.

"I had a hard time controlling Joab," he told her. "And keeping them from discovering my casket room in the cellar. They already suspect I'm mad and that would have finished it."

"Have you any ideas about who it might be?" she asked.

Barnabas had a grim look on his handsome face. "Yes. I think I know who it is now," he said.

Rita's eyes opened wide. "Who?"

"Clifton Kerr," he said quietly.

She was stunned to silence. At last she said, "Why Kerr?"

"It all fits so neatly," he said with some excitement. "Kerr was stricken with some strange African disease. He couldn't face sunlight. Then Moreno treated him just as he's treated me and he came back to normalcy. Kerr must have been placed under some voodoo curse as I was, or bitten by a vampire bat to cause him to become one of the living dead. Moreno had learned the secret of the serum during his years in Africa, and he made his witch doctor's formula pay off handsomely. He's built Kerr into a star and kept him completely under his control."

Rita listened to it all. "But why should Kerr suddenly revert to his vampire state now?" she asked.

"I don't know the answer to that," Barnabas admitted. "Unless Moreno deliberately withheld the serum from him so he'd go out and attack these girls at night. And so place suspicion on me. It could be an effort to make you stay in line."

She frowned. "Clifton Kerr came after me the other night and kissed me against my will. I thought he was behaving oddly, as if he had been doped or something."

"He was high on blood," Barnabas said in a hard voice.

"I believe you're right," she agreed. "And that's why he hasn't been reporting for work. He's been sleeping off his nighttime adventures."

"Probably in a coffin they have stowed away somewhere in the bowels of that boat," he said.

"Moreno is engineering it all," Rita said helplessly. "What are we going to do?"

"I'm going to face Dr. Moreno and ask him what his game is," Barnabas said. "There has to be a showdown."

"I'm going with you," she insisted. "I introduced you to Moreno in the first place."

Barnabas stared at her in alarm. "I'd rather you didn't," he said. "I don't know what the outcome will be."

"I want to be there," she insisted.

They left the house and made their way directly to the path leading down to the wharf. A policeman stationed at the entrance of Collinwood eyed them warily but did not challenge them. The fog still was heavy and its dampness seemed to pervade everything. As they neared the wharf the wash of the waves became louder punctuated now and then by the dirge of the Collinsport foghorn from a distance.

She stayed close to Barnabas as they approached the big pleasure craft. "Do you think the doctor will be aboard?" she asked in a low voice.

"I'd say so," Barnabas told her.

The deck of the boat was wet from the fog and slippery, as if some oil might have been spilled on it. They made their way to the doctor's cabin and Barnabas knocked on it.

Almost at once Dr. Moreno opened the door. He stared at them without showing any surprise. "Guests at this early hour," he said.

"The police have probably already been here," Barnabas said.

The doctor smiled. "You are quite right. They have. We had a most interesting discussion. Won't you come in and be comfortable."

Rita seated herself on the green divan but this time Barnabas remained standing as did the doctor. Barnabas began, "I'm here for a direct talk. I know who killed that girl. It was Clifton Kerr."

Dr. Moreno regarded Barnabas with amusement. "You must tell the police that. Then they'll surely believe you're insane. They're only half convinced of it at the moment."

"There's no use bluffing," Barnabas said. "You recognized my disease because you had treated it before. Kerr was a vampire until you helped him and now for some reason of your own you're allowing him to revert."

Doctor Moreno stared at him. "You realize that no one would even listen to such a fantastic story."

"Because of my own position I know what I'm saying is true," Barnabas declared.

"Very well," the doctor said with a shrug. "Just for our own ears I'll admit you've hit on the truth. Clifton Kerr is suffering from the same condition as you."

Barnabas said, "I knew it. Why have you held back the serum from him?"

The doctor smiled coldly. "I haven't. I know you'd enjoy making me the villain in all this. But that doesn't happen to be the case."

Barnabas frowned. "What are you saying?"

"I'm telling you that Kerr has been indulging in his vampire orgies because he enjoys them," the doctor said with relish. "You see he is not as noble as yourself. Few are. He likes a smooth throat and warm blood. With him it has the same result that a three-day spree has for an alcoholic. He's willing to be a normal human being most of the time as long as he can enjoy these occasional lapses. I have no choice but to go along with his wishes. Of course he is not able to work when he is indulging his more bestial nature but the spells fortunately do not last long."

Rita looked at the doctor accusingly. "You allowed him to murder that poor girl."

"Not at all," Moreno said smoothly. "It happened and I had no control over it. She's not the first one he's killed. He sometimes gets carried away and behaves too violently."

"I never killed when I could avoid it," Barnabas told the doctor.

"As I said before, you are a person of character, Mr. Collins. I regret that Clifton Kerr has little, if any. But that is the way it is."

"He must be stopped," Barnabas said. "He can't go on like this."

"He'll report for filming tomorrow, I promise you," the doctor said. "This particular lapse has ended. He is sleeping it off now."

"But he'll revert again," Rita protested, "and murder someone else."

"Who can say that?" Moreno demanded. "This may be his final lapse. I always have the serum available when he desires it."

Barnabas's face was stern and his deep-set eyes regarded the sinister doctor accusingly. "You know he will revert again and you don't care," he said. "You'll let anything happen as long as you can control him and the money he earns for you."

"That's a very nasty statement, Mr. Collins," the doctor said with mock regret. "If I hear much more of this from you I shall feel forced to cut off your supply of serum. And you know what that will mean."

Barnabas clenched his fists. "I'm no longer sure I want it."

Doctor Moreno gave him a cynical look. "I can only tell you, Collins, that I'm the sole person in America who can provide you with this serum. The sole person in all the white world. And you would not know where to seek the information in the jungles of Africa. A secret which I stumbled on by a lucky accident."

Rita stood up and took Barnabas by the arm. "He's right," she said worriedly. "You mustn't quarrel with him. He's our only hope."

The doctor looked pleased. "You have always impressed me as a most sensible girl, Miss Glenn."

"I'm being suspected of what happened," Barnabas said. "You know that."

"The excitement will pass in a few days. They can prove nothing," the doctor said airily. "You have no need to worry as long as I provide you with the serum."

"Kerr must be stopped," Barnabas warned him. "You do it or I will. I'll not be party to allowing a murderer free to prey on society."

"Kerr is a most valuable property," the doctor said. "I have no intention of seeing anything happen to him. I bid you both good day. I have other urgent matters to attend to." He went over and held the cabin door open for them to leave.

Not until they were making their way up the path to the top of the hill did Rita ask, "What are we going to do?"

"I don't know yet," Barnabas said with a sigh. "We'll have to be patient."

Rita was in a state of dread when she reported on the set the next morning. The fine weather had returned and Brad Hilton had quickly taken advantage of it to get his cameras and lights and sound trucks lined up for a sequence at the cliff. It was one of the most important scenes in the film and included bits by most of the principal actors.

Clifton Kerr, looking smug and assured, had been one of the first to make his appearance. Rita avoided looking his way whenever she could. But she knew that soon she would have to do a scene with him. Dr. Moreno hadn't come to watch and that surprised her. Brad was in a hard mood to satisfy and kept repeating small bits of action.

At last it came time for her to appear before the cameras with Kerr. At once she had to acknowledge that his murder spree had at least improved his acting. He played the difficult scene with her with more reserve than usual. And she was forced to exert herself in keeping up to his pace in playing. When they finished, Brad approached them with a smile.

"That was just great," he said. "So good we don't have to make a second take. We'll move on to the argument between Billings and Shaw."

As Rita left the set Clifton Kerr followed her. "What did I tell you?" the leading man asked in a mocking fashion. "I've always said we'd make the greatest team."

She kept her back to him. "I haven't anything to say to you," she told him.

"That's a great mistake," Kerr mocked her. "Because I have a great deal to say to you. For one thing, Moreno and Hilton are having a council of war at Collinwood tonight. I'll be on the yacht alone. The two crewmen are on holiday. I'd like to take her out for a moonlight sail. A private voyage for just the two of us. Doesn't that sound cozy?"

Rita gave him an angry look. "Do you think I'd even consider such a thing?"

"I think you might," the leading man said in his arrogant fashion. "I know a lot of girls who'd like the same invitation, but I'm reserving it especially for you."

"It's not appreciated," she said sharply.

"The doctor is leaving the boat around nine," he said, as if she'd accepted. "Come anytime after that. I'll be waiting."

"It could be a long wait!" she warned him and wheeled around to stride off and join Blanche. They went back to the house for her to remove her costume and make-up.

Kerr's conceit angered her all the rest of the day. She did not have a chance to talk to Barnabas about the incident because he didn't appear on the set. And the afternoon was devoted to other outdoor location scenes which kept her too busy to visit him at the old house.

After dinner one of the state policeman came for a talk with Brad Hilton. She watched nervously as they retreated to the study and closed the door after them. She wondered if any new clues to the murder had turned up and what they might be discussing. And she especially worried if the police were still looking on Barnabas as their chief suspect.

As soon as she could she left the house and started through the yard toward the old house. She'd only gone a little way when she met C. Stanton Shaw on the path.

The old character actor paused to say, "I've just been down to the old cemetery for a walk. I found it a fascinating place. Many of the tombstones had interesting inscriptions."

"Yes, I've been there," she said.

He gave her a wise look. "By the way, your friend Barnabas Collins was down there. He's quite an authority on the family history. We had a pleasant chat and I left him there, but I suspect he may be on the way back now."

She thanked him and hurried on. As she neared the crest of the hill overlooking the cemetery she saw the familiar figure of Barnabas in his dark caped coat coming toward her. He was carrying his silver-headed black cane and walking swiftly. At once she knew a feeling of relief.

When he came up to her she quickly told him of the happenings of the day and especially of Clifton Kerr's arrogant behavior. She ended with, "I believe he's convinced I'll join him for a trip on that yacht tonight."

Barnabas looked at her with a strange expression in his deep-set eyes. "That's exactly what I want you to do," he said, surprising her completely.

CHAPTER 10

Rita stared at him. "I don't understand."

Barnabas's face became sternly set. "It's the only answer. Clifton Kerr has to be destroyed. And you can help me do it."

She was shocked by his words. "You mean murder him?"

"If you want to call it that," Barnabas said wearily. "There is no other way. In spite of Moreno offering to allow him to live a normal life he has developed a thirst for blood. He enjoys being a vampire when it suits him. You can see how it fits in with his arrogant, maniacal nature. To all intents Clifton Kerr is a dangerous maniac and a threat to the community while he remains at large."

"Can you kill a vampire?" she asked in a whisper. It was a question she had often pondered. Barnabas had lived as one for more than a century and he should surely know. There must have been attempts on his life during that long period.

"There is only one way," he said. "You must be the decoy. Once we get him out in the boat I'll attack him. A hawthorn stake must be driven through his heart. Then his body will decompose rapidly. It is best done during the day but tonight the full moon will serve almost as well. Ordinarily the body should be burned, but we can dispose of it in the ocean."

Rita was aghast at the way Barnabas was coolly planning it all, and yet she knew that he was right. He was doing what should be done. Her own experience with the leading man had shown her that he was beyond reforming. He had no desire to change his vampire state as Barnabas had. He was, as Barnabas had said, a threat to innocent people.

She gave a great sigh. "I don't know," she said. "I'm not sure that I can go through with it."

Barnabas touched her arm. "You'll have no part in the violence. Merely go aboard as he asked. I'll have stowed away on the boat in the meanwhile. After we are out a distance from the shore, things should develop naturally."

She frowned up at him. "But how will we explain his death?"

"You can say he tumbled overboard on the way back," Barnabas said. "Everyone knows he drinks a lot. It's the type of accident that could easily happen. You'll somehow moor the boat at the wharf in an amateur way and then raise the alarm at Collinwood. You're an actress. You should be able to carry it through."

Rita was amazed at his calm planning. "I'll not have to act," she told him ruefully. "I expect I'll be in shock."

"Kerr will kill again if we don't move now," Barnabas said solemnly. "He may even attack you tonight. And he would leave a guilty trail which would eventually implicate me and spoil any chances I have of living a normal life again."

"But what about Moreno? He'll know."

"He won't be sure. He may guess."

"And if he does he'll not be willing to go on giving you the serum," Rita pointed out. "So you lose no matter which way it goes."

Barnabas shrugged, a determined expression on his handsome features. "I know about Kerr, so I have no choice. I'll have to take my chances with Moreno."

Rita's eyes were filled with fear and she said, "I don't want you to revert to what you were. I don't think I could stand it now."

"Moreno will have to listen to reason," he told her. "It's only a matter of time before Kerr will get him in trouble. He's smart enough to know that."

"But if he doesn't? If he blames you and refuses you the serum?"

Barnabas looked bleak. "Then I will have to leave here. Say goodbye to Collinwood and you."

"No," she pleaded. "I don't want you to leave no matter what happens."

"It's too early to worry about that," he said. "We have a night of trial ahead. And first we must find a suitable hawthorn piece and fashion a stake from it. I think there's something I can use at the old house."

Rita went back with him to the ancient stone building and waited in the somber and dust-laden living room while he sought out the hawthorn stake in the cellar. The room was laden with a ghostly atmosphere, heavy with the tragedy of the past. The great drapes at the windows were rotted with dampness and the windows themselves so streaked with dust and covered with cobwebs that little light filtered in.

About the evening's plans she was of a divided mind. It was as simple as a struggle between right and wrong, with Barnabas representing the moral side. But could you murder and still be moral? Would Barnabas wind up ruined by his attempt to prevent the mad Kerr from killing again. Surely Clifton Kerr was well advanced in insanity or he would not deliberately revert to his vampirical acts. And it would not be a murder in the true sense since Kerr had really died when he'd been bitten by that bat in Africa years ago. Since then he'd been living as one of the walking dead.

Barnabas had no qualms about removing Kerr from the scene because he knew what the vampire curse meant. And he was positive now that Kerr had no intentions of changing his ways. She worried more about Moreno than she did Kerr. Moreno would be vindictive. He was greedy and was making a fortune from the actor's earnings. He would not be swayed by the knowledge that his partnership with the arrogant Kerr was leading him to eventual trouble. He would only consider the immediate loss.

Perhaps if she talked to the sinister doctor she could make him see this other side of it. It was a forlorn hope but at this time she was ready to clutch at anything. And every minute it was getting closer to nine o'clock when she was supposed to present herself on board the boat.

Night was descending and by the time Barnabas appeared in the wide doorway of the living room again she was sitting in almost complete darkness. His broad-shouldered figure loomed in the shadows and he held up a barely visible object in his hand.

"The stake is ready," he said quietly.

She got up. "Barnabas! I'm frightened!"

"Don't be," he told her, coming to her. "I'll go ahead now. By the time you reach the boat I'll be hidden aboard. You have nothing to fear. I'll be close to you every minute you're there."

She stared at him in the shadows. "You're determined to go through with it?"

"Kerr has made anything else impossible," he said. "You shouldn't be sitting alone here in the dark."

"I won't stay after you go," she said. "I'll walk slowly

back to Collinwood and then go down to the boat to keep my appointment."

"It will be all right," Barnabas promised her and he gently touched his lips to her forehead.

She strolled back to Collinwood after he left her. Her mind was in a state of confusion. In addition to the fear that something might go wrong there was her revulsion to what they had planned and to cap it all her sheer terror of the unscrupulous Dr. Moreno. He controlled all their destinies since he possessed the serum.

As she came close to the entrance of Collinwood she heard a footstep behind her and turned to see the blond young actor, David Billings. The young man came up to her with a sheepish expression on his fine-featured face. "Rita, I've been wanting to speak to you," he said.

"Yes," she halted, trying to hide the strain in her voice.

"I want to apologize if I've caused you any annoyance," he said quickly. "I know I behaved foolishly in blaming you for the fact my role was cut down."

"It doesn't matter," she told him tonelessly.

The actor looked worried. "But it does," he insisted. "Your dresser, Blanche, seems to have the idea I even tore up a photograph of you."

"I asked her not to mention that."

"I'm glad she did," David Billings said. "It gave me a chance to tell her she was on the wrong track. If anyone tore that photograph it was Clifton Kerr."

"Clifton Kerr?" she couldn't hide her surprise.

"Yes," the actor went on. "That night I met him in the upstairs hall coming from the direction of your room. And he certainly didn't have any reason for being up there. He's a vindictive person and he'd do it thinking I'd be blamed just to cause trouble."

"I'm ready to forget it," she said. She didn't bother to explain her own theory that the photo had been destroyed by a phantom.

"That's generous of you," Billings said. "But I want you to know I had nothing to do with it. And I realize now that it's Kerr who is causing all the trouble about the script. I just saw his so-called agent, Dr. Moreno, going into the house now for a meeting with Brad. I suppose that means a lot more script changes and Kerr's part being padded."

"It will work out," Rita assured him, grateful to know that Moreno had left the boat and was actually in Collinwood at that moment.

"I guess we'll have to put up with it," the young actor said bitterly. "Clifton Kerr is the big name in this production and he's going to have things his way."

"Please don't worry any more about the photo," she said as she prepared to move on.

"Thanks," Billings called after her as she walked on in the darkness.

She carefully made her way down the path leading from the cliff. The moon was beginning to lighten the night shadows now and she could see that the yacht was ablaze with light. As she made her way toward it a new thought was troubling her.

What would Brad do about the film with Kerr gone? He had only shot a few of the scenes. There were a number still to do. Would it mean the end of the picture? Or could Brad find some way to complete the project without the leading man? She knew most of the intimate scenes and close-ups had been completed. It was mostly the action shots that remained to be done.

It was a macabre business! She was on her way to a rendezvous with a man the effects of whose death she was already debating. And she was conscious of a chill even though she'd donned her heavy tweed coat. The deck of the boat was deserted when she stepped aboard.

But a moment later Clifton Kerr emerged from his cabin, clad in slacks and a white shirt open at the neck. She saw at once that he was either drunk or having one of his insane spells. He actually appeared unsteady on his feet as he gravitated toward her.

He took her hand in his and the clammy coldness of his flesh made her shiver. With one of his overbearing smiles, he eyed her, saying, "I knew you'd come."

She raised her head a trifle defiantly. "I didn't make up my mind until the last moment."

"Rubbish!" he said. "You decided the very second I invited you. I don't like girls who play hard to get." And he weaved over to the moorings and untied the boat before he leered at her drunkenly again. "We'll have plenty of time to talk when we get out where we can have some privacy. I don't want dear Dr. Moreno coming back and butting in."

Rita watched with frightened eyes as he slowly went about starting the engine and heading the boat out from the wharf. The cove and the ocean beyond seemed deserted at the moment. The light at Collinsport Point flashed its beam across the calm surface of the water occasionally. There wasn't a hint that Barnabas was aboard , and she began to fear that she was alone on the craft with this madman.

Kerr remained at the wheel for a short time and then switched it to automatic steering and came over to where she was standing. He attempted to put an arm around her. "I think it's time to go down below where it's more comfortable," he suggested, leering at her.

She stepped back. "Please! Let me be!"

Kerr took on an ugly expression. "You accepted my invitation, didn't you?"

"And I expected you to behave like a gentleman!"

"Like your Barnabas Collins, maybe?" he said with biting sarcasm as he reached for her again.

"We can leave Barnabas out of this," she told him.

"Glad to," Kerr said with his eyes fixed on her and a strange, burning glitter in them. "So you like the vampire's kiss, little Rita. Well, you may be interested to know that Barnabas isn't the only one Moreno is feeding his serum to. I can give you that same kiss! And I know your blood will be sweet!"

She gradually became aware of his intention. She saw the beads of cold perspiration at his temples, the fixed staring look in his eyes, his slightly opened mouth with his perfect white teeth partly exposed. He made a surprise move and grasped her roughly. She screamed out her terror and attempted to beat him back, but it was too late! He had her in his powerful hands, and with a demonic expression of delight he brought his lips to her soft, white throat.

She was still screaming when Barnabas loomed up behind Clifton Kerr and brought a wooden mallet down on his head, sending him slumping to the deck unconscious. Barnabas stepped over his prostrate figure to take her in his arms.

"Are you all right?"

She nodded. "I didn't think you'd come."

"I was waiting for the right moment," he said, and he released her to give his attention to the figure on the deck. Staring at the crumpled form, he told her, "I can't allow him to come to."

"So it's now?" she whispered.

"Now," he said firmly.

She watched as he produced the slim stake of hawthorn and turned Clifton Kerr's body over so that his chest was exposed. The actor's face held an evil expression even in his stunned state. Barnabas glanced at her as he poised the stake in his left hand over the actor's heart. Then he raised the mallet.

"You'd better not watch," he cautioned her.

She clasped her hands over her face and held her breath as she heard the several thumps of the mallet. And when she allowed herself to look again the stake had been driven through Kerr's body and blood was gushing from the wound it had made. And at the same time the actor's entire frame was withering. His face had taken on the worn look of a very old man and his hair had turned white.

Barnabas tossed the mallet overboard. Then with a haggard

look at her he bent down and picked up the decomposing body and tossed it into the sea. There was a splash and it vanished.

He looked at her. "It's done," he said in an agonized tone.

"I hope we were right," she said in a low voice.

"We had to be," he assured her. "Now I'll clear the traces of this blood from the deck and then we'll head back to the wharf. Prepare yourself to tell your story."

She moved to the railing and watched the lights ashore as Barnabas cleaned up the evidence of what they had done. Kerr had proved he was a menace in the very last minutes he'd been alive but she still was shaken by what they had been forced to do. She knew that soon she would have to make her way up to Collinwood in frantic haste and tell a story of a supposed accident in which Kerr had toppled into the ocean. She expected everyone to believe her but Moreno.

It was Moreno she feared, not only for his reaction towards her but for what he could do to Barnabas. If he chose to withhold the serum now it would only be a matter of a few hours or days at the most before the man she loved reverted to becoming the same loathsome thing they'd just destroyed. Not that Barnabas had ever been like Clifton Kerr. Even as a vampire he had lived by the gentleman's code he had known in life. With the actor it had been vastly different.

The lights of Collinsport blinked in the distance. She could imagine it was another busy night in the village. The Blue Whale would be crowded. The coming of the picture company had swelled the population of the village and there were also some regular tourists who'd managed to find accommodations. Then her gaze moved along the shore to Collinwood standing stately on its high hill overlooking the cove. There were lights blazing from most of the windows of the mansion. Brad would be there and Moreno with him.

Barnabas came up beside her and stood silently for a moment. At last he said, "We'll be heading back now."

"Yes," she said in a whisper.

"Think you can manage it as I instructed you?"

"I'll do my best," she told him, and gave him a frightened glance. "I'm worried mostly about you. What will happen to you?"

"It will be all right," Barnabas promised.

She knew that he was merely trying to stop her from being too filled with despair. There was no telling what would happen from now on. It depended entirely on Moreno, and he was one of the most cruel men she had ever known.

The return trip to the wharf seemed to take a surprisingly short time. As they neared the shore Barnabas told her, "I'll just loop a single rope on the dock, barely enough to hold her. As if you'd done it."

As soon as the boat touched the wharf he helped her off. Then he held her in his arms for a brief moment and their lips touched. "Be brave," he whispered as he left her to vanish in the darkness.

Rita stood there on the wharf a moment, dazed by the swiftness of it all. And then she began to sob. It was no acting on her part. The gruesome evening was taking its toll. Still sobbing she stumbled from the wharf and made her way up the path to the cliffs. She hurried awkwardly across the lawn toward Collinwood and reaching the door pressed the bell quickly several times.

Brad Hilton answered the door himself. And the moment he saw her the director took her in his arms. "Rita, what is it?"

"Kerr," she sobbed. "He fell overboard."

The director's grip on her became more tense. "You're hysterical! It can't be!"

She nodded numbly. "We went out for a while. He was drinking. I couldn't do anything with him. He fell overboard just before we reached the shore!"

"Moreno!" The director shouted over his shoulder to the man inside and then rushed out into the darkness, apparently on his way to the boat to see if her story was true.

The sinister doctor came stalking out onto the steps beside her, his swarthy face livid with rage. It was clear he had heard her. In the moment before any of the others rushed out he murmured, "You vixen!" And deliberately raised his hand to give her a punishing welt across one side of her face and then the other.

The ferocity of his blows combined with her frantic state to send her into blessed unconsciousness. Vaguely realizing what had happened to her she collapsed in a heap on the steps.

When she opened her eyes Blanche was bending over her, anxious and holding smelling salts under her nose. "Are you feeling better?" the older woman wanted to know.

Rita rolled her eyes wearily. She felt terribly tired. "Yes," she whispered. She saw that she was stretched out on the fourposter in her own room.

C. Stanton Shaw was close by at the foot of the bed and his face showed annoyance. "Don't worry any more about it, Rita," he said. "If it wasn't for the picture I'd call it good riddance to bad rubbish."

She raised herself on an elbow. "Where's Brad?"

"Down below," the old actor said. "There are a lot of things to be looked after. The police have to be informed and the newspapers. We'll have the place swarming with reporters by tomorrow."

She closed her eyes for a moment. "What about Moreno?" she asked in a small voice.

"He's in a rage," Shaw said caustically. "But then, that doesn't surprise me. He's always complaining about something. He seems to want to blame you for what happened. But don't listen to him."

"I could do nothing," she said dully. "Clifton Kerr was responsible for his own destruction."

"You never spoke truer words," the old actor said.

"I think she should be left alone to rest," Blanche said.

"I agree," Shaw said. "I just wanted to bring her up-to-date. The best thing for her now would be a couple of sleeping tablets."

But even the drug of the tablets did not prevent her from having nightmares. Time after time as she tossed under the sheets of the four-poster the weird, demon face of Clifton Kerr in those last moments came back to haunt her. The burning eyes filled with madness and the slavering lips finding a place on her throat were all part of the grotesque episodes of her troubled sleep. She moaned and cried out against his attack and then she opened her eyes wide and sunlight was streaming into the big bedroom.

Brad was standing beside her bed staring down at her intently with his one good eye. "I'm sorry if I woke you," he apologized.

"No, it was a dream," she said. "A bad dream. I was on the point of waking anyhow."

"I can imagine you might have a lot of bad dreams for a while," the director said dryly. "I wasn't as involved as you were and it's an evening I won't soon forget."

She closed her eyes for a second. "It was dreadful!" she said.

"Later the police will want to ask you some questions," Brad said in his reassuring tone. "It's nothing to worry about. Merely a routine in accidents of this type."

"I understand," she said.

"I don't know where the film stands," Brad admitted with a wry look on his face. "The grounds are crowded with reporters. It will take at least a day to clear the air of them. Hollywood has been phoning through the night and morning. I'll have to make some arrangements for a memorial service in the local church. We'll restrict it to the company so as not to make a circus of it."

"That would be wise," she agreed.

"Clifton was out to kill himself," Brad said bitterly. "He had a greater desire for self-destruction than anyone I've ever known. He was never a normal person from the time he suffered that fever in Africa."

"What about Moreno?"

"He's retreated to the boat in a rage," Brad said with some relish. "He's lost his power over the company now, and as you can imagine he's not taking it too well. I don't think he cared anything about Kerr except for the money he could make from his efforts."

"I'm sure you're right," she said.

Brad sighed. "In spite of Kerr's staying away when he liked, we managed to get most of the inside scenes and the close-ups finished. There's an outside chance we can finish the picture by using a look-alike to stand in for Kerr in the long shots."

"I hope so," she said. "I know how much you've put into this film."

"There's always risk," the director said. "Nothing in life is sure. We'll wind up the location scenes with the others here and then I'll go back to Hollywood to work on the stand-in parts. We can shoot it just as well there and I'll have more technical talent available."

"I'm sorry it all turned out this way," she said listlessly from her pillow.

"As long as you are safe," Brad said sincerely. "You take it easy for the day. Better to keep out of the way until we can get rid of the reporters." He started for the door and then paused to turn and tell her, "Oh, yes, Barnabas Collins came by a little while ago to ask about you. I told him you were still sleeping."

"Thanks," she said, gratified and relieved to know that Barnabas had put in an appearance.

As soon as Brad left she went back to sleep again, and it was not until late afternoon that she dressed and went downstairs. Things had quieted a good deal. Most of the press had vanished and Brad was in town looking after some important details, according to David Billings. She was filled with a strong desire to talk to Barnabas and decided to walk over to the old house and see if she could find him.

The door of the old mansion was ajar and she mounted the steps and peered in. Almost immediately Joab appeared from the shadows and stood there looking at her with pure hatred on his ugly, beard-stubbled face.

She said, "Is Mr. Collins at home?"

He snarled at her and advanced on her threateningly. She quickly stepped back. Either Barnabas wasn't in the house or he was there and ill. Joab always behaved in that fashion when he was standing guard over him.

She hurriedly went down the steps and as far as the crest of the hill. But there was no sign of Barnabas in the isolated cemetery near the pine trees. And then she had a sudden realization of where he must have gone. He was surely on the boat with Dr. Moreno.

Once the thought had seized her she forced herself to walk down to the wharf. A trembling came over her as she neared the boat but she knew she had to conquer this and brave the situation for the sake of the man she loved.

Approaching the door of the cabin, she knocked on it. There was the sound of movement from inside and then Moreno opened the door. His swarthy face took on a fresh look of loathing as he saw her.

"I wouldn't expect you to come here," he said.

"I'm looking for Barnabas," she told him.

Moreno smiled coldly, the eyes behind his dark glasses showing his hatred. "He has been here," he said. "And he's gone."

She stared at him anxiously. "Is he all right?"

Moreno said, "What you're asking me is, did I give him his regular dose of serum?"

"Yes," she said.

The doctor smiled grimly. "I have good news for you. I gave him his injection."

She felt a surge of relief. It was going to be all right in spite of everything. "Thank you, Doctor."

"I need no thanks," Moreno said. "He paid me, but as I explained to him, there will soon have to be a slight adjustment in my fees. With Clifton Kerr gone I have lost a major source of income. So my fees are bound to be higher."

CHAPTER 11

S he said, "How much higher?"
    "I haven't quite decided that," the doctor said in his suave fashion. "It will depend on a number of things. But you can be certain that my terms will be reasonable."

Rita couldn't hide her hostility for the dark man as they stood there facing each other. With contempt she said, "I can guess what your idea of reasonable might be,"

The doctor smiled coldly again. "It's too bad you have such a dislike for me, Rita. I could be a good friend to you."

"I can manage without your friendship," she said.

Moreno sighed. "I suppose you are still angry because I struck you last night. Please try to understand that it was the emotion of the moment. I was unable to control myself, and I deeply regret that I so violently assaulted you."

"I'd call it your true nature showing."

"You see," he said. "You are prejudiced. You will not even consider my apology."

"I have said nothing about what you did," she reminded him. "I think that is about all you have a right to expect."

"And I have appreciated your silence," he said with one of his oily smiles. "It is a most promising sign."

"I don't know what you mean by a sign," she said.

"We can't guess what lies ahead for us, just as poor Clifton had no idea of the fate that was in waiting for him. It may seem strange or even ridiculous to you now, but I have an idea we may one day become close associates."

"I doubt that very much," Rita said coldly and she turned and walked away from him.

As she reached the top of the cliff she saw Brad getting out of one of the station-wagons. He was smoking his straight-stemmed pipe and wearing gray tweeds. She realized with some surprise that he would have been quite a good-looking man if it weren't for the black eye-patch. In a way, however, that gave him a jaunty appearance. And he wasn't all that old. Certainly on the right side of fifty.

As he reached her he took his pipe from his mouth and said, "What were you doing down there?"

She managed a grim smile. "You know the old theory. A murderer always returns to the scene of his crime."

Brad looked grim. "I'm not asking for wise answers," he said. "I'd be interested to know what could possibly attract you to that boat after last night's tragedy."

"I went down looking for Barnabas," she said. "I haven't been able to find him."

"I saw him in the village in the general store," Brad told her, his single eye fixed on her shrewdly.

"Then he should soon be back," she said.

"He should be," Brad agreed. "I wonder if you're being honest with me. If you really went down there looking for Barnabas or to have a talk with our mutual friend, Moreno."

She tried to appear innocent. "Why should I do that?"

"That's what has me bothered," the director said evenly. "He's lost Kerr and I wouldn't be surprised if he started looking for some other talent to control."

Rita shook her head. "Not me. I promise you. You needn't worry about that."

"I would worry if it happened," Brad told her with great earnestness. "Remember, Moreno is clever. Don't think you can outsmart him or you're apt to wind up the loser."

"I simply asked him if Barnabas had been down there," she said, trying to evade Brad's close scrutiny.

"Why should Barnabas Collins visit Moreno?" Brad asked.

Rita blushed. "I think I explained before. Moreno gave him some medical advice."

"And if I remember correctly I told you Moreno was a charlatan to be avoided," Brad told her. "Collins seems too intelligent to me to be taken in by him."

"I've told you the truth," she said. "You can believe me or not. And anyway, I don't think you have any right to question me this way. I'll tell the police what I know when they ask."

She took a step past him towards the house. "Rita!" he called after her.

She stopped and turned around, at once hurt by the look of pain she'd brought to his deeply honest face. She tried to be casual. "Well?"

"I don't think you should talk to me on that level," he said. "I have always tried to be your good friend."

"I'm sorry," she said, meaning it.

Brad looked glum. "It's all right. And I suppose I was talking out of turn. But every time I know you're with that Moreno I get upset."

"I know," she said.

"He's no good, Rita," Brad told her. "You know how he interfered with our shooting schedule. I wouldn't be in the fix I'm in now if he'd allowed Kerr to report for work regularly as he should have."

"You don't have to warn me against Moreno," she said.

"I think I do," Brad worried. "In spite of what you know he has a way of getting around people. You're a valuable show property and I can't believe he hasn't got his avaricious eyes on you this minute."

"It will do him no good," she said.

Having said that, she went on inside. She was deeply troubled by the strange attitude of Dr. Moreno's and knew that he must have some new evil scheme in his mind. But what? He'd given Barnabas the serum without any argument and this proved that he had something else planned and was only waiting for the proper moment to spring the trap on them.

Of course Brad was right. Moreno was not to be trusted. But she could not tell Brad the truth about Barnabas. She could not tell anyone. That was the power Moreno held over them. Soon the police would be questioning her and she would have to somehow continue to make her account of what happened sound plausible.

Because of her nervous state she would have preferred to avoid dinner. But there was no escaping it since she didn't want the others to know how tense she actually was. Little was said at the table, which was a blessing from her standpoint. Even Brad sat quiet and with a worried expression on his weathered face.

After dinner as she was passing through the hall on her way to the living room she was accosted by C. Stanton Shaw. The old man studied her with his bright eyes and a sympathetic expression.

"I hope you are feeling better," he said.

"I'm still not quite myself," she told him.

"That's to be expected," he agreed. And then, nodding to the portrait of Barnabas on the wall of the hallway, he went on, "I've been taking a most extraordinary interest in that portrait."

"Yes?" she said faintly.

"Surely you must have noticed," the old man said, giving her a sharp glance. "It bears a striking likeness to Mr. Barnabas Collins. I believe this is a painting of one of his ancestors."

Rita gazed up at the somber face so skillfully depicted in dark oil tones of another age. To protect Barnabas she felt forced to say, "I don't believe I had noticed the likeness until you mentioned it."

"Amazing," the old man said. "I call it more than that. Uncanny. This present young man from England is a complete physical throwback to the subject of that painting."

Rita was anxious to get off the subject and away from the old man. She said, "I must speak to him about it."

"You should," Shaw said, his face alight with the pride of his discovery. "I've done a good deal of delving into the family history and come up with some amazing facts. This is a house of tragedy and ghosts, you know."

"Really?"

"Indeed," the old man assured her. "And there has been more than one suicide at that cliff. I tell you the Collins family has not had a happy history."

"So I understand," Rita said in a dull voice.

"I think it is not strange that this tragedy in the company should happen here," the character actor went on. "Collinwood seems to shadow any who live within its walls with evil luck. Of course, Clifton Kerr was living on the boat and he surely was gradually edging towards destruction. But I think it is revealing that his death should have taken place here."

"It's something I'd rather not dwell on," Rita said.

The old man looked apologetic. "Of course. I'm sorry. I allowed myself to be carried away. Please forgive me."

At least it silenced him and he allowed her to go on into the living room where she sat alone by the window. She was hoping that Barnabas would soon come by. There were so many things she wanted to talk to him about. And she couldn't help agreeing with Shaw that Collinwood was indeed a place of dark shadows. Fear and concern had haunted her since she had come to stay there.

But it wasn't Barnabas who first arrived. When the entrance bell at Collinwood rang it was an officer from the headquarters of the state police. He was a colorless man of middle height dressed in plain clothes and wearing a trench coat and no hat. Brad brought him in and introduced him to her.

"This is Inspector Freeze of the state police," the director said. "He has come to talk to you."

Rita was rigid with fear but she forced a smile as she rose to greet him. "Thank you for waiting so long to question me, Inspector. I've had a bad day."

"To be expected," the police official said, shaking hands with her. "It's more an account of what happened that I want than to question you," he said, taking out a notebook and pencil.

"I'll do my best to make it clear to you," she said, seating herself in the tall-backed chair again and sitting there nervously with her hands clasped in her lap.

Brad, who had taken a stand to the left of her chair, told the Inspector, "Miss Glenn was not a close friend of Mr. Kerr's. She just happened to have gone with him for a short trip on his boat last night."

"So I understand from Dr. Moreno's account," the inspector said as he sat opposite her with the notebook open and the pencil posed. "If you'll just give me a general outline of the events from the time you got aboard to when you arrived back here to give the alarm," he suggested.

Rita began in a voice with a tremor in it. The inspector did not at any time interrupt her but kept busy making voluminous notes in what appeared to be shorthand. When she had finally come to the point of her breaking the news to Brad and ended the account, he sat back frowning at his notebook.

"I think that covers it," he said at last. He gave her a sharp glance. "You felt he had been drinking or taking some powerful drug from the time you stepped on board."

"Yes," she said. "As soon as I saw his condition I regretted that I had accepted his invitation."

The inspector continued to study her closely, his plain face betraying no expression. "But it was too late then."

"He cast off almost immediately," she said.

Brad spoke up. "Clifton Kerr had a wild, reckless nature. He was given to excesses of all kinds."

Inspector Freeze accepted this without comment. He gave his attention to Rita again. "After he fell overboard you somehow managed to get the boat back to shore and docked."

"He'd already set it on course and I had been watching what he was doing," she said carefully. "I'd been worried that he might pass out and I'd be left with the responsibility of getting back."

"And you were all alone on the boat with him?" The inspector's colorless eyes were fixed on hers.

She had a moment of panic but she fought it. "Yes. We were

all alone on board," she said.

"You showed remarkable calm and ability in mooring the craft as well as you did," the inspector said.

"Rita is one of the most intelligent young women I've ever worked with," Brad said, putting in a word for her.

The inspector appeared thoughtful as he folded his notebook and returned it and the pencil to an inner pocket. "I'd be inclined to agree with you. Not many young women would have kept their heads as she did."

She swallowed hard. "I knew I somehow had to get to shore and let them know. I hoped he might perhaps still be saved."

"A natural reaction," the inspector said dryly, "though you realize now the chances of that were minimum."

"Yes," she said in a low voice.

The inspector stood up. "Well, I think that will be all for now, Miss Glenn. We may want to talk to you later, although I hope it won't be necessary."

"Thank you," she said, rising, hers very directly.

"It must have been a shocking experience for you. You have my sympathy. To be on board with him alone when that happened."

"It was," she murmured.

"If there had only been someone else with you," he said and then shrugged. "Probably then it would never have happened. Thank you, Miss Glenn."

She stood there staring after him as Brad chatted with him and showed him out. She felt the last statement of the inspector had been a trick one. She was certain that he suspected there had been someone else aboard. That she and an accomplice had murdered Kerr. That it hadn't been an accident at all.

Would he return to probe some more? To keep playing a cat-and-mouse game with her until he had caught her up in some detail and was able to charge her with Clifton Kerr's murder? She almost believed it could work out that way. She was positive he doubted her story. She wished fervently that she could tell him the truth and explain that Kerr was a monster preying on the community. But who would listen to her tale of vampires?

"I think you satisfied him," said Brad, who had come back to join her.

"I hope so."

"He's pretty upset," the director went on. "There have been all those attacks on young women in the neighborhood. Then the murder of our script girl and now this drowning accident. I guess he wishes we'd go back to Hollywood."

She gave him an urgent look. "When will we be leaving, Brad?"

He shrugged. "Just as soon as I can finish the few extra scenes that have to be taken in this background. All the ocean shots of the slave ship will be done off the California coast."

"I hope it's soon," she said. "I've never been so anxious to leave a place."

"I can understand that," he agreed. "We have a lease on Collinwood for the balance of the summer but we won't remain anywhere near that long. Probably another week will wind us up."

She gave him a wan smile. "Thanks for standing by while the inspector was here."

"It was the least I could do," Brad said.

"Apparently he'd talked to Dr. Moreno before he came here," she ventured.

"Yes," Brad said. "Moreno is bound to be an important witness. I wonder how long he plans to remain here. I have no doubt Kerr's estate was left to him and so the boat is his."

"No doubt," she said grimly.

The entrance bell rang again, and this time it was Barnabas. She felt a great flow of relief at the sight of him. Brad spoke to him briefly and then made a discreet withdrawal to the library.

Barnabas came into the living room and took her hands in his. His eyes scanned her face concernedly. "You look ill!"

"It's all right," she protested. "Now that you've come. It hasn't been an easy day. The police were here just now to see me."

"Oh?"

"I told them what I could," she said, giving him a significant look and knowing that he was aware of the possibility of their being overheard by others in the house. "I feel he was satisfied."

Barnabas's deep-set eyes told her that he understood. "That must have been an added ordeal."

"It brought it all back again."

"I know."

She said, "Perhaps I'd feel better if I had some air. We can take a walk."

"An excellent idea," he agreed.

It was growing dark and she got her coat since the air would be cool now. They quickly left the house and walked across the lawn in the direction of the cliff. Not until they had reached the jutting cliff and sat on the bench there did they talk freely, sure that they had complete privacy at this isolated spot.

Barnabas was worried. "Do you think the police are suspicious?"

"I think so," she admitted. "They seem to doubt that I was able to land the boat by myself."

"I should have dived from the boat and swum back,"

Barnabas fretted. "Then you could have remained out there until they came to rescue you."

"I couldn't have stood it and it would have meant a long swim for you," she said. "You handled it the best way."

"I hope so," he said grimly.

"They've accepted my story. They may wonder about it, but how can they prove anything?"

"They've been dragging for Kerr's body," he told her. "They'll never find it of course. Its disintegration would become complete shortly after it sank under the water."

"You feel certain of that?" she eyed him curiously.

"I know it."

"We'll just have to wait," she said. "Brad claims we'll be working on the picture another week before we leave. I don't know when Moreno is going."

Barnabas frowned. "He didn't give me any clue. In fact he behaved strangely when I saw him. I'm sure he knows what happened, but he made no mention of it and gave me the serum."

"He told me he did," she said. "And he said something about his having to increase his fees."

The man on the bench beside her sighed. "I feel certain he's planning some terrible revenge on us."

"And so do I," she said unhappily, grasping his arm. "Oh, Barnabas, how can we escape from this?"

He patted her hand gently. "Let me do the worrying," he told her. "I can stand up to him."

"Not if he withdraws the serum."

"I don't think he has that in mind," Barnabas said. "He's planning something else."

Darkness was complete now and it was a night without stars. But there was the beam of light from the Collinsport lighthouse and the cluster of tiny dots of light on the other side of the cove marking the village. Down below at the wharf the boat showed a glow through the portholes of the doctor's cabin.

"He's remaining aboard," Barnabas said, staring down at the craft.

"He behaved weirdly when I talked to him," Rita recalled. "He was threatening in his manner and yet he actually predicted that we would one day become allies."

"I hope not," Barnabas said sharply.

"It's utterly ridiculous."

"Still, he must have had something in mind."

Rita sighed. "Brad has warned me against him. He has an idea Moreno may try to get me to take him on as my agent now that he's lost Kerr."

"He doesn't have the hold on you he had on Kerr," Barnabas pointed out.

"Brad doesn't know that," she said. "He doesn't guess what Kerr was or anything about you needing the serum."

"Brad is a fine man," Barnabas said sincerely. "I'm glad he's around to watch over you."

"I don't need him now that I have you," she said, gazing at Barnabas with loving eyes.

Barnabas looked at her solemnly. "It is important to me that you have someone else. There are times when I feel that I can never adjust to this age or become a proper mate for you."

"Barnabas!"

"It's true," he went on bitterly. "I'll always be a slave to the serum. At the mercy of Moreno."

"New discoveries may be made. This arrangement with him could turn out to only be a temporary thing," she protested.

"I'd like to believe that," Barnabas admitted. "But we don't know."

"Nothing is sure in this life," she countered. "Unless it is my love for you, and I will not have you deny that."

His arm went around her. "You know I would not lose you without a struggle. But we must face facts. At the moment we don't know what Moreno may be up to."

"We should find out soon enough," she said.

"Let us hope his demands aren't too unreasonable," he worried. "I shudder at turning back into what I was before."

"That mustn't happen!"

"We'll not worry about it as long as he keeps giving me the serum," Barnabas said. "But don't make any alliance with Moreno against Brad. It is Brad you must depend on and whom you can trust."

"I realize that," she said quietly.

"If Moreno decides to return to Hollywood I'll follow," Barnabas said with a frown. "I'm tired of being here. There are too many memories. And the old house repels me now that I am normal again."

"I think it would be best for you to leave," she said.

"We'll trust that the police don't bother you anymore," he went on. "And that I can come to terms with Moreno. Once those things are settled we'll know what our future together can be."

Barnabas saw her back to Collinwood. A strange, high wind had come up, making the water of the cove rougher than usual. The waves were pounding a dirge on the shore as he kissed her goodnight. Rita felt a certain mournfulness in the air and for perhaps the first time she had the feeling that she might be losing

Barnabas. His handsome face wore a look of infinite sadness as he left her to stride off in the shadows towards the old house.

Letting herself into the silent house she mulled over what he had said. She'd been startled by his mention that he found it difficult to adjust to this new age and the people in it despite his great love for her. She paused to stare up at the ancient portrait of him in the dimly lit hall and it struck her how much the lone wanderer had experienced through the years. How many periods he'd lived through, the heartbreaks he'd known and the always present ordeal of his being shut off from normal life and a fugitive much of the time.

Unlike Clifton Kerr he had fought the curse and tried to control his thirst for blood. But it had stalked him until Moreno had sold him his series of injections. Barnabas had lived so long that he was weary and the estate with its memories of the curse and lost romance was surely not a good place for him to remain.

With a sigh she went upstairs to her bedroom. She was awakened in the middle of the night by the big hinged windows in her room blowing open. They burst open to let the clamor of the eerie windstorm fill the room. It awakened Blanche also and at once she rose and rushed over to close the windows. Then she drew the drapes again and came over to Rita's bedside.

"Were you awakened, Miss Glenn?" the buxom woman asked.

"Yes," Rita said. "The window couldn't have been properly latched."

"I don't understand," Blanche said as she went back to her own bed. "I was certain I had carefully looked after it."

Rita stared up into the darkness, pondering on the strange gust, and as she did so she became aware of the pervading scent of violets in the air again. The perfume was sickeningly strong, so much so that she wanted to cry out and draw Blanche's attention to it, but she was afraid that the older woman would deny the scent existed and dismiss it as a nightmare.

But she knew differently. She shivered and drew the sheets tightly to her as she looked into the shadows. She had the feeling that the windows flying open had signaled the entrance of an angry spirit. The spirit of the long dead Josette came to tell her she would not win after all, that in the end Barnabas was to be lost to her. With this despairing thought she fell asleep.

The next day the weather was fine and warm. Brad at once urged the technicians into action and had a series of scenes underway before noon. He was working at a feverish pace now in his anxiety to get the necessary sequences completed and leave the gloomy estate.

Rita had scenes with both David Billings and C. Stanton Shaw. They went well enough, although in some cases Brad, with his usual desire for perfection, insisted that they be repeated.

It was shortly before the lunch hour, when she was resting in a chair a short distance from the set, that she saw Dr. Moreno striding across the lawn towards her. The swarthy man wore one of his smartly tailored gray suits and was looking smug.

Coming up beside her he smiled and said, "I trust the picture is going well, Miss Glenn."

"It seems to be," she said cautiously.

"I understand Brad will soon have the work here finished," he went on. "I suppose we shall soon all be saying goodbye to Collinwood." He paused significantly. "With the possible exception of your friend Barnabas."

"If you go to Hollywood I believe Barnabas will move out there as well," she said.

"Indeed," he said, the eyes behind the dark glasses cold. "Then he plans to continue as my patient. Very flattering for me."

"You know he needs your help," Rita said, looking up into the sarcastic doctor's face.

"About that," Moreno said. "I have finally decided on my terms, and I'd like you to come down to the boat this afternoon when you finish working. We can have tea or cocktails and I'll tell you what I have in mind."

CHAPTER 12

Rita recalled the warning Barnabas had given her about having anything to do with the unscrupulous doctor, and she said, "I don't believe I can make it."

"You had better," he said. "If you know what is good for your friend."

"My actions have nothing to do with him," she declared.

"On the contrary," he said. "Say we make it around four thirty?"

She stared at him, stunned by his assurance. She knew he was holding withdrawal of the serum from Barnabas as a threat over her head, and it was her fear for Barnabas that made her say, "I'll try to be there."

Moreno nodded and moved on. She saw no more of him during the rest of the day. He was not popular with the company and now that Clifton Kerr was gone he rarely showed up when they were filming. She worried about what to do and almost confided her problem to Brad, but she knew the director would strictly warn her against a meeting with the doctor, and Brad did not understand the weakness of her position since he knew nothing of Barnabas needing the serum.

They finished her scenes at four o'clock and as soon as she had changed from her costume she quietly made her way to the path and down to the boat. Dr. Moreno was waiting for her and seemed in an excellent humor. He had provided a tray of tasty items to eat and her choice of drink.

Sitting primly on the green divan she told him, "I can't stay long. Please tell me whatever is on your mind."

Moreno stood before her, the eyes behind the dark glasses bright with malicious humor. "I can't say there is much charm in your approach."

"You know I am here only because you've forced me to come," she said.

He looked pained. "Now, that is an unfortunate way of expressing the situation. I would rather say you have come to ensure that I will continue to minister to your good friend Mr. Collins."

Rita said, "To put it plainly you suggested you'd stop giving Barnabas the serum he needs to keep him normal unless I came."

"I suppose that is a fair summing-up of it," he admitted. "And don't you agree I have that right?"

"I know you have somehow happened on a miraculous remedy but you have misused your knowledge. You allowed Clifton Kerr to become a moral decadent so you could make a slave of him. You controlled his talent and used it to make a personal fortune while you allowed him to slowly deteriorate."

Moreno's swarthy face took on a grim look. "That is a rather strong accusation."

"You know what I say is true."

He eyed her coldly. "And isn't it also true that you and your precious friend Mr. Collins deliberately caused Kerr's death. You murdered him on this boat and made it seem an accident. Suppose I told the police that?"

"Then you would also have to reveal that you let a monster prey on unprotected girls in the area. That you were a collaborator in his murdering one of them."

He sneered. "I doubt if that unfortunate episode would come into it."

"But you daren't take a chance, do you?" she defied him. "Barnabas rid the world of Clifton Kerr because he had become an uncontrollable menace and there was no other solution."

"Barnabas is as much a vampire as Kerr ever was and with the same thirst for blood," the doctor reminded her sharply.

"Barnabas has fought the curse. Kerr reveled in it. There's a big difference."

"I didn't bring you here to argue Barnabas' merits," he said. "I have had you come here to learn my decision concerning his treatment."

"You can't be so cruel as to withhold help from him now?"

The doctor took a sip of the drink in the tall glass he was holding. "I'll be happy to go on treating Collins," he said, "providing the fee I want is paid. I only make up the serum as it is used. It must be fresh. And it's costly."

"Aren't you asking him enough now? How much do you expect?" she demanded angrily.

"I expect something more than mere money," Moreno said smiling at her over the tall glass. "I lost a valuable property in Kerr. I need someone else to replace him. I propose that it shall be you."

She jumped up. "Me?"

"Yes. I'd like to manage your career as I did Kerr's."

"Never!"

He raised a hand to quiet her. "You haven't heard me out yet. I think the best way to arrange it would be for you to marry me."

This time she couldn't answer. Her eyes opened wide. "You have to be joking!"

"I'm extremely serious," he insisted. "I've given this a lot of thought. We'd make a wonderful team. I can boost you higher as a star than you've ever been before. And, of course, my gratitude will extend to Mr. Collins, whom I'll continue to treat."

"So that's your price?" she asked grimly.

"I don't expect you to make an immediate decision. Think it over for a day, even two. I'm sorry but that is as long as I can wait. If you haven't made up your mind by then I'll have to refuse to see Mr. Collins."

"That's blackmail!"

"Whatever it is, I think we could be happy together," he said. "And you do want to see Mr. Collins living a normal life."

She stood up. "I'm sorry. You're wasting time."

"I didn't expect to have you agree to my suggestion now," he said. "But I'm sure you will later when Mr. Collins goes a sufficient time without the serum only I can provide."

She paled at the thought. "If it's only more money you want I'll make it up."

"No." He shook his head. "I don't think you properly understand me, Rita. I'm as much interested in power as I am in money. Power over a particular individual. I have a sizable fortune now. I don't really need extra money that badly. But I am a very lonely man and that is where you come in."

Her eyes flashed at him angrily. "You know I could never love you or marry you!"

"Love is something that can grow between two mature people," Moreno reasoned with a smile on his swarthy face. "I'm positive you'd come to care for me in time."

"And if I did agree to such a ridiculous arrangement," she said, "what promise would I have that you would continue to doctor Barnabas?"

"I have thought about that," he said. "It would be simple enough. I'd allow you to send the airmail parcels of the serum here to him every two days. There is no reason why he couldn't administer the hypos to himself."

"Then I would not be allowed to be near him?"

"I'm afraid not," Moreno said. "I realize there is a certain unhappy attachment between you two. Time and distance can cure it. But it would never do to have him live near us."

Rita regarded the man in the gray suit with disgust. For the first time she noticed that his hair was streaked with gray and that he was squat and ugly, actually a little shorter than she was. Most of the time she had avoided giving him a close scrutiny. But in the light of his proposal she couldn't help but look at him with different and more appraising eyes. He was as evil-looking as his nature.

He apparently took her silent moment of staring at him as a good sign. He said, "Be generous, Rita. I'm a lonely man. Share your life with me."

"I'll try to forget we ever had this talk," she said and started out.

"And I'll try to forget you helped murder Clifton Kerr," he said coming after her. "And I'll be generous when you come back begging me to marry you."

She gave him a bitter look over her shoulder. "Don't count on it!"

She hurried from the deck of the yacht and along the wharf. She was still fuming with rage and despair as she walked up the path to the cliff. She had expected Moreno to demand some vast sum of money from them, but she had never guessed anything like this.

Yet, as she slowly made her way across the lawn to the house, she knew that he had won. He had predicted exactly right. Rather than see Barnabas revert to his lonely and macabre vampire existence again she would make the sacrifice of marrying this man she despised.

Once she'd ruined her life in that manner, her career would mean little to her. The fact he'd also become her agent and manager wasn't all that important. And even suicide would be no escape from him, since it would surely mean the end of things for Barnabas. Once she'd married Moreno she would have to go on living with him.

She didn't know why she hadn't agreed to his suggestion at once. It was her spirit which had caused her to rebel, but she loved Barnabas too much to let him down. And she wouldn't dare tell him her reasons for marrying Moreno or he'd refuse to allow her to go through with it. Perhaps the best thing was to say nothing for a few days. To let Moreno wait for his answer and keep the whole thing a secret from Barnabas. That was her final decision.

But she hadn't anticipated the ruthlessness of the man she was dealing with until several nights later when she and Barnabas took a stroll in the direction of the old cemetery. Brad was planning to use it for a final scene the following morning and she wanted Barnabas to point out some of the oldest tombstones to her.

Brad's technical crew had been at work and wires and cables streaked in among the cemetery stones, while tall banks of lights, camera booms and sound cranes had been arranged around the quaint burial ground with its spiked iron railing. In the field near it were some generator trucks and the whole array was in contrast to the isolated spot on the edge of the forest.

As she and Barnabas made their way through the cemetery gate he suddenly halted and leaned heavily on his silver-headed cane. She stared up at him in surprise and saw that his face had taken on its old sallow appearance and great beads of perspiration were standing out at his temples.

"Are you ill?" she asked quickly.

The man in the black cape coat shook his head. "No. It's just a passing something. I'm all right now." With an obvious effort he braced himself to stand very straight and they moved on into the cemetery.

One of his first stops was before Josette's tombstone. He stared at it with somber eyes and at the same time asked Rita, "Did you ever smell the scent of violets in your room again?"

A chill crept through her. She studied his handsome profile as he stood there absorbed in the gravestone. "Yes," she said in a small voice. "The other night the windows blew open in an unexplainable manner and afterward there was the same perfume in the air."

He nodded silently. "She was my first love, you know," he said. "She and I would have lived a happy normal life but for Angelique and her curse. I can understand that she is restless in her grave."

And now he gave Rita a sharp look. "You have had someone sleep in your room with you as I suggested?"

"Yes, my maid Blanche."

"Do that until you leave here," he advised her as he turned

to study the gravestone again. "There is a secret room off one of the vaults here," he said. "I have never shown it to you. But in the old days I sometimes used to go there."

"An underground room in this place?" she asked with a touch of horror in her voice and disgust on her pretty face. It at once brought to mind a dark place crawling with insects and rank with the fetid odor of death.

Barnabas gave her a significant glance. "I know the thought is repulsive to you. And I will not show you the room. But try to understand that I did not mind it. There was peace for me there. The world of the dead is a separate world. And I was part of it."

"Please don't say such things," she begged.

"I must be truthful," he said simply. And waving to indicate the many ancient tombstones around them he went on, "Under each of these stones lies someone I once knew. Someone who experienced passion, sorrow, joy and ambition. Who lived their day and died as I was forbidden to do. There are times when I cannot help envying them!"

Rita touched his arm. "It has all changed for you now," she said.

And once again she knew that no matter how despicable a marriage with the sinister Dr. Moreno might be she would go through with it. She had to save Barnabas from returning to what he'd described as the world of the dead.

He moved about the cemetery explaining who was buried at various spots so that she might pass on the information to Brad in the morning when they began filming. He suggested what he felt might be interesting angles of the old burial ground and for a time seemed quite himself.

Then as they were about to leave he seemed to take another attack of pain again. This time he rested against an above ground vault and touched the back of his hand to his eyes.

Rita was really upset now. There had to be something wrong. "Barnabas, tell me, what is bothering you?"

He lowered his hand and stared at her with dull eyes. "The serum," he said. "He's refused it to me for three days now."

"Why didn't you tell me before?" she demanded.

He did not answer her at once, leaning forward and grinding his teeth as if undergoing excruciating pain. When the spasm was over, he gasped, "Not your worry."

"What did he say to you?" she demanded angrily.

"He kept putting me off. Telling me to come back each day. I've been in torture," Barnabas admitted. "I cannot survive the night without either the serum or blood."

Rita listened to him with growing consternation. "But he

had no right to treat you that way," she said. "He was supposed to go on giving you the serum unless I refused him. It was part of our bargain."

Barnabas suddenly stood up, a questioning look on his handsome face. "Unless you refused him what? What bargain are you talking about?"

She took a frightened step back, aware that she'd betrayed herself. She said, "It will be all right. I'm going to him now."

He came quickly toward her and for someone who had been so stricken he seized her arm with surprising strength. "I want the truth!" he cried.

"Barnabas, you're hurting me!"

"What bargain?" he insisted.

She looked up at him tearfully. "It's all arranged. He's to go on treating you and I'm to marry him."

Barnabas stared at her incredulously. "You're to what?"

She repeated it, then said, "Please don't try to change anything. I've made up my mind!"

"Rita, don't be a fool!" the man she loved said. "You know I won't let you go through with anything like that! And anyway, Moreno has no intention of going on giving me the serum. He won't keep his part of the bargain."

Rita was sobbing pitifully. "Barnabas, what are we going to do?"

He let her go and stood staring into the growing dusk. "What I should have done in the first place. Have a showdown with Moreno."

"What kind of showdown?"

The handsome man in the black cape gave her a strange look. "I have not lived for more than a century without learning how to deal with scum like Moreno. We'll go see him."

Rita was distrustful of his new tense mood. She hesitated, "I think you should wait."

"I've told you I can't wait," Barnabas warned her. "I've already reverted. I can feel the tug of the dead world pulling at me. When the moon rises tonight I'll be thirsting for blood."

Her pretty face was a mask of terror. "I don't believe it."

"That's the way it was before," he said quietly. "Come along with me. There's a last chance Moreno may decide to give me the serum. And I want to straighten out any ideas he may have of making you his wife."

Despite her protests she found herself leaving the cemetery and walking at his side as he headed toward Collinwood and the wharf on the beach below. He was striding with great speed and she could barely keep up with him. A new vigor seemed to have taken hold of him.

It was close to dusk as they passed Collinwood and headed across the lawn to the cliff and the path leading down to the wharf. As they went down she saw there were lights on the boat. Moreno was undoubtedly there and probably alone since the crew members were still on holiday and none of the picture company cared to associate with him.

Barnabas was moving ahead of her and as they reached the wharf she tugged at his arm and pleaded, "Please be careful."

He glanced at her. "It will be all right."

They reached the cabin and he raised the silver-headed cane and pounded the door with it. Moreno opened the door and gave them a look of mild surprise. "I didn't expect a visit from you both," he observed.

"This won't take long," Barnabas said, forcing his way into the cabin.

Moreno stood back with an ugly look on his face. He told Rita, "I'm not much impressed with your friend's manners."

"A good match for your ethics, Dr. Moreno," Barnabas snapped as he stood facing the squat, ugly doctor with Rita at his side.

"What does this mean?" Moreno demanded.

"I want some of the serum," Barnabas said. "Enough for a dose now and enough so that I can give myself shots when I need them."

A nasty smile crossed Moreno's face. "Save your strength and nerves. You'll need them before this is over."

Rita spoke up, "You promised to supply him until I'd given you my answer."

Moreno looked pleased. "And what is your answer?"

"I'll marry you whenever you like just so long as you save him," Rita declared.

Barnabas raised a hand to draw her back and told the doctor. "She's talking wildly. There'll be no marriage. I want the serum and now without any of your dirty bargaining."

"It's no good, Collins," Moreno said in his hard way, the cold eyes behind the dark glasses fixed on him. "I've made up my mind. I made it up when you finished Kerr. Rita is the only one who can save you by becoming my wife."

"That's your final answer," Barnabas said slowly.

Moreno said, "It's my only answer."

Barnabas hesitated a moment. Then he turned to Rita. "I want you to leave us. I have something private to discuss with Moreno."

Panic filled her again. "No," she argued.

"You must," he said firmly and, propelling her to the door, pushed her out onto the darkness of the deck and slammed the door in her face. She stood there bemused and then heard the angry voices of the two men from inside. After a moment Moreno gave a loud frightened cry.

The cry roused her from her stunned state and she rushed over to one of the portholes and stared into the cabin. The sight that met her eyes was not a pretty one. The powerful Barnabas had seized the squat doctor and his teeth were buried in the sinister man's throat. Rita gave a cry of horror and averted her eyes from the awful sight. She sagged against the side of the cabin thinking she would faint.

She did not know how long it was before Barnabas came out of the cabin and found her. He took her arm with great gentleness, but there was stern purpose in his voice as he told her, "We must get away from here at once."

Allowing him to lead her up the path she tried to close her mind to what she had seen in the cabin. She tried to tell herself that she'd imagined it, that everything was all right. Still, she didn't dare ask him about Moreno.

At last they arrived at the door of Collinwood. Barnabas seemed on edge, saying, "I must say goodnight."

She stared up at his pale handsome face looming above her in the darkness. "What happened?" she whispered.

"He won't bother us again."

"And the serum? Did he give it to you?"

"It's all right," Barnabas said. "You mustn't worry. I'll manage."

"I'll see you in the morning," she said. "After we finish the scenes at the cemetery. You'll join us there, won't you?"

"I'll be somewhere there," he promised.

"Oh, Barnabas!" she said with a sob and she came close to kiss him goodnight.

He held her back a little. "Not on the lips," he said quietly. And he touched his own lips to her forehead and for the first time in a long while she realized they were ice cold.

Before she could remark on this or ask him any more questions he had turned to walk off in the darkness. She stood staring after him with a terrible feeling of desolation. She tried to persuade herself that he had overpowered the evil doctor and obtained the serum so that he would be himself again in the morning. It always took the serum a time to work when he'd been without it for a period. Thinking this, she turned and went inside.

C. Stanton Shaw was coming down the stairs as she went up. The old man offered her a smile. "There'll be a full moon tonight," he said. "The kind of night for lovers."

"Yes," she said faintly, avoiding his eyes and holding onto the rail.

"But also a night for other things," the old man rambled on. "A night for werewolves, banshees and the walking dead. A night for phantoms of every sort who prefer the pale moonlight to the bright day. And I vow you'll find more of them here at Collinwood than you will lovers." He chuckled at his own joke.

"I'm going to bed early," she said, excusing herself as she prepared to go on upstairs. "We'll be starting early with those cemetery scenes in the morning."

"The proper place to end the wretched time we've spent here," the old man said. "In the cemetery. I'll not be sorry to leave this strange mansion with its legends."

She said a polite goodnight and went on up to her room. She was glad that Blanche was not a garrulous person like Shaw and she quickly prepared for bed.

Brad had them all at the cemetery at nine thirty the next morning. She gave him the information about the various sections of the burial ground which she'd learned from Barnabas and Brad plotted his scenes. The filming took up the entire morning.

As noon drew near and they were about finished she began to wonder where Barnabas was. He'd promised to drop by but so far he hadn't. At last Brad finished the final take and ordered the crew to dismantle the technical equipment. The location work at Collinwood had come to an end.

The director went over to Rita and said, "All that's left to do now can be done in Hollywood. And with only a few rewrites to take the Clifton Kerr role out of some of the action scenes I think we'll be able to complete the picture and make it a good one."

She was on her feet. "I hope so," she said.

He glanced at the cemetery. "Those scenes we made here this morning will lend lots of atmosphere. I want to thank Barnabas for his advice. By the way, where is he?"

"I don't know," she said fearfully, her eyes wandering up to the forbidding old house atop the hill. "He said he'd be here."

"We'll likely see him later," Brad said. "I'll drive you back in my station wagon."

Lunchtime passed and still there was no word from Barnabas. Everyone was packing to leave. They were driving to Bangor for an early evening flight. Some of the technical crew were driving the sound and generator trucks back to New York and Brad had sent word to Vermont that the Collins family could return anytime.

He told Rita, "I'd like to have you meet that Victoria

Winters. She and Barnabas seemed to get along well. She took me to his place the first time I met him."

Rita said nothing. She was too upset and wondering what could have happened to the man who had captured her heart. Then the dreadful news broke like a doomsday knell. It happened when one of the crew returned to the boat and then came hurrying up to Collinwood in an agitated state.

"Moreno's dead," he informed Brad as a pale Rita stood beside him. "I found him just now. Must have had a heart attack or something."

After that it was a nightmare. The police came again. Rita had a vague remembrance of sitting in the living room with Brad and others of the company and being interrogated by the same colorless Inspector Freeze.

The inspector said, "I'd say that Moreno died from natural causes. There were no signs of violence. No marks on him at all except for a curious red scar on his throat that could have come from careless shaving or almost any kind of abrasion. One odd thing, the coroner says there was hardly a drop of blood in his body. He must have been suffering from some debilitating disease for a long while."

When the inspector had gone Brad said to her, "Well, they say there are always three deaths. Moreno makes the third one."

She gave a tiny shiver. "Brad, take me to the old house. I want to try and talk to Barnabas before we leave."

"I'd forgotten about him," the director admitted. "We'd better go now before we eat. We'll be leaving soon after."

"Yes," she said in a tiny voice.

The sunshine of the morning had vanished and the fog was moving in swiftly, pulls were flying close to shore and uttering their melancholy calls. Brad gazed up at the sky with his one good eye and worried about the weather and if their flight would be able to take off on schedule at Bangor.

Rita began to tremble as they approached the steps of the house and saw that the oaken door was closed and the windows tightly shuttered. "Try the door," she asked Brad.

He went ahead and used the knocker. When no one answered he tried the handle of the door and it swung open. He turned to her. "It's not locked," he said. "But I don't think Barnabas can be here. Or that Joab either or he'd be out here snarling at us by now."

She said nothing but pushed past him, almost racing into the dark hallway to the living room and then to the other rooms in the dusty, murky old house. They were all empty.

She returned to the wide doorway of the empty, ruined

living room and stood there staring at it with her eyes brimming with tears.

"He's gone," she whispered.

Brad slowly came to her side. "I'm sorry, Rita," he said with great sincerity. "I know how much you cared for him. But he's a strange fellow. It mightn't have worked out. Perhaps he decided it was best."

She nodded. She was sobbing and unable to make any proper answer.

Brad put an arm around her and began guiding her towards the front door. "I don't think you should take it this way," he said. "Perhaps one day you'll meet again. After all, it's not as if he were dead."

They had reached the steps now. Brad closed the door after them and with his arm still around her guided her down the steps. They began the slow walk back to Collinwood.

She kept thinking of what Brad had said! It's not as if he were dead! And it was true. That was the one hope. Somewhere, she knew, Barnabas was still alive. And if he was lost to her he might once again come upon a chance to save himself as he almost had with Moreno's serum. She checked her sobbing.

The man with the black eye patch smiled down at her and said, "I'm no handsome bloke like Barnabas, Rita, but remember I'll always be around."

She looked up at him with gentle eyes and knew that this could be truer than either of them realized. Hadn't Barnabas himself told her, "Depend on Brad."

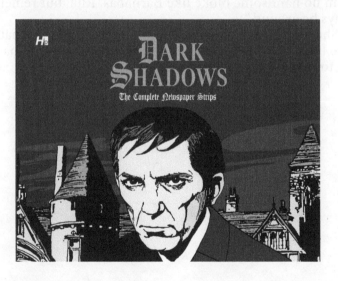